GHOST FROM THE GRAVE
A CHANTILLY ADAIR PARANORMAL COZY MYSTERY

CAROLYN RIDDER ASPENSON

GHOST FROM THE GRAVE

Copyright © 2020 Carolyn Ridder Aspenson.

All rights reserved.

No part of this book may be reproduced in any form or by any electronic or mechanical means, including information storage and retrieval systems, without written permission from the author, except for the use of brief quotations in a book review.

Severn River Publishing
www.SevernRiverPublishing.com

This is a work of fiction. Names, characters, businesses, places, events and incidents are either the products of the author's imagination or used in a fictitious manner. Any resemblance to actual persons, living or dead, or actual events is purely coincidental.

ISBN: 978-1-64875-024-3 (Paperback)

ALSO BY CAROLYN RIDDER ASPENSON

The Lily Sprayberry Realtor Cozy Mystery Series
Deal Gone Dead
Decluttered and Dead
Signed, Sealed and Dead
Bidding War Break-In
Open House Heist
Realtor Rub Out
Foreclosure Fatality

Lily Sprayberry Novellas
The Scarecrow Snuff Out
The Claus Killing
Santa's Little Thief

The Chantilly Adair Paranormal Cozy Mystery Series
Get Up and Ghost
Ghosts Are People Too
Praying For Peace
Ghost From the Grave
Deceased and Desist
Haunting Hooligans: A Chantilly Adair Novella

The Pooch Party Cozy Mystery Series
Pooches, Pumpkins, and Poison
Hounds, Harvest, and Homicide
Dogs, Dinners, and Death

The Holiday Hills Witch Cozy Mystery Series

There's a New Witch in Town

Witch This Way

Who's That Witch?

The Angela Panther Mystery Series

Unfinished Business

Unbreakable Bonds

Uncharted Territory

Unexpected Outcomes

Unbinding Love

The Christmas Elf

The Ghosts

Undetermined Events

The Event

The Favor

The Magical Real Estate Mystery Series

Spooks for Sale

Selling Spells Trouble

Cloaked Commission

Other Books

Mourning Crisis (The Funeral Fakers Series)

Join Carolyn's Newsletter List at
CarolynRidderAspenson.com
You'll receive a free novella as a thank you!

To Jack
For always believing in me

CHAPTER 1

Olivia poured me a tall glass of her delicious sweet iced tea, a secret family recipe. In my opinion, the recipe—and the tea—were the best in the state. I was the only one she'd chosen to share it with, and I appreciated that, but I wouldn't risk making it myself. Some things are better left to the professionals.

She sat at the small table in the old kitchen of the Castleberry Georgia Historical Society where we worked. "Did you talk to the board?"

"You know how the board is. There are rules for a reason, rules can't be changed, this is the integrity of our community and the history of our town at stake. Oh!" I held up my finger. "And my personal favorite. If it's not in character with the era, it's not worth discussing. That's why they hired me." I gave her a big, toothy smile. "Yay, me."

"The power trips are crazy. So glad I don't have to deal with them."

"Be careful. That's coming." I swirled my drink in the glass. "Of course they're right, but they're not the ones telling the residents they can't change their homes. They won't budge on this one."

"I don't see why not. The verandah is stunning."

"I agree, but it's not in keeping with the home's design." I picked at a cheddar biscuit from Community Café, our friend Del's place. I wanted to shove the entire thing in my mouth, but I convinced myself not to. Del's biscuits are the size of softballs and have the calorie count of an entire farm of extra-crispy fried chicken, which is why they're so good. I took my time with it, savoring each small bite like it was my last.

"What're you going to tell Mr. Bennett?"

I sighed at the thought of that conversation and also because I knew I'd end up eating the whole biscuit. "I'm going there this morning. I just have to pull some photos of other Civil War-era homes to bring along. I hope with that and my design suggestions I can convince him to go with what the board wants, or at least something close, which I might be able to get them to approve."

"What about the pool?"

"I don't see that happening. Pools were only for the wealthy back then."

"Not just back then."

I smiled. "Still, I can't see the board changing their mind on that."

I'd been the Castleberry Georgia Historical Society Manager for three years, and most of the time, I loved the job. Olivia and I worked well together and had become good friends even though I'm just a few years younger than her mom. I loved the desire by most everyone to keep Castleberry's history alive. The board? Meh, I could do without them.

I'd moved back home from Birmingham, Alabama, with my then-tweenaged son after a tough divorce from the man I thought I'd spend the rest of my life with. Austin and I moved into my childhood home, the one my parents kept preserved just like it had been when I was a kid. They'd passed a few years ago, and at first, I kept the home almost completely as they'd left it, but with some encouragement—AKA pressure from Austin—we'd just finished a complete remodel. I loved the place both ways, but I missed that childhood-home feeling.

"You were able to change your place, and you did it in keeping with the character of the community," Olivia said.

"But my house isn't a historical property."

"I know, but it attests to your commitment to the community and to making sure things stay within its character. The board should know that."

"It's not my commitment they're worried about. It's John Bennett's lack of respect for pretty much everything they want. He's a bully."

She leaned forward and whispered, "He does act like someone's peed in his grits every time I see him."

I laughed. "I can name five people who've probably done that."

John Bennett didn't choose Castleberry, his ex-wife did. Like me, she moved here with their son after the divorce, and when she let him know they'd landed here, he packed up and left Boston without looking back. And he'd never let anyone in town forget it.

He's a Northerner through and through, and our Southern hospitality hasn't rubbed off on him yet. It's a common issue in small towns like Castleberry. It takes some time for the rush and tension of living in the north to wear off, but once it does, those Northerners relax and enjoy our laid-back lifestyle. The problem is really less about them and more about the ones born and raised in the South. Sometimes we forget to give our new friends a chance to chill out and get used to us. Our friendliness can be quite overwhelming.

But the problem with John Bennett wasn't just an adjustment issue. He just hadn't tried to become part of the community.

Instead of involving himself and making an effort to be friendlier, he'd chosen to be the rebel without any consideration for abiding by Castleberry's unwritten rules, let alone making an attempt to get to know the community or anyone in it.

"He'll come around," I lied.

"You have a lot more faith in the world than I do," she said, winking at me.

Olivia's personality had blossomed over the few years we'd worked together. I certainly didn't want to take credit for it, but I did hope a small part of her new confident persona came from my example. "You're so bitter in your old age."

"I'm almost thirty now," she whined. "I'm practically a spinster."

I rolled my eyes. "You do know that's not a thing anymore, right?"

"What, being old and single?"

"It's okay to be older and single." I emphasized the *er* in "older." "But the word spinster implies cranky and bitter."

"Have you met Delphina Beauregard?"

"Del doesn't count."

She laughed. "You just made my point."

Del would, by definition and implied meaning, be a spinster. She wore a permanent scowl and scared most everyone in town with her grouchy personality, but buried deep underneath that scowl—and I mean really deep—was a kind heart.

"She's our friend and she would die to help her friends, so she gets a pass." And if she did die, she'd better come back as a ghost or I'd be pitching a fit the size of one of her homemade biscuits. Del knows how I feel about that because she knows I can see the dead.

Shortly after I moved back home, I tripped on the stairs at work and hit my head on the floor. I still don't know exactly what happened, and the three MRIs I've had show nothing at all, but ever since that tumble, I've been able to see ghosts. Yup, real and very dead apparitions practically everywhere I go. I've since done a lot of research and become friends with another woman who sees spirits. She's helped me through the maze of the afterlife, and I am eternally grateful. No pun intended.

Only a few spirits have actually needed my help. The goodbyes I've delivered for some were both heartbreaking and satisfying. Angela, my psychic medium friend, says spirits just want to finish their business here on earth and then happily go to the other side, but most of my experiences have been different, and I'm grateful for that. The emotions of final goodbyes take a toll on me. They're exhausting. But unlike Angela and her work, most of the spirits I come across don't want to go to the other side. They're happy to stick around and walk among the living. Maybe Castleberry is their little piece of heaven?

When the dead need me, they don't usually speak to me directly. They lead and guide me along a path so I can both help resolve their business and deal with a situation in my life. Sometimes they'll show me bits and pieces of their lives or how they died. I've learned those experiences usually have a double meaning. They're somehow related to something I'm dealing with, and like a thousand-piece puzzle, it takes time to put the pieces together.

Watching the moments before a person took their last breath can be scary. But for reasons I'm not sure I'll ever understand, I've been given a skill to help them, and I do the best I can.

I do have one regular spirit who comes around quite often, one who speaks to me, and I know for certain he has no desire to leave. Charlie is waiting for my friend, his wife Thelma. As much as I love that woman, when it's her time, I'll be happy for her. They miss each other something fierce.

"Are you going to talk with him?" Olivia asked.

I'd been lost in my own thoughts. "With who?"

"Bless your heart. You're pretending you don't know what I'm talking about. Jack Levitt, that's who."

I hadn't said more than a "hey" or "see ya" to Castleberry's one and only police detective in two weeks, and I had no plans of being the first to start a conversation. "I'm not pretending anything. I was thinking about the ghosts in town. But no, I'm not going to talk to him. What's done is done, and that's all I have to say about that."

"What's that expression? It ain't over till the fat lady sings? Yeah, that."

I furrowed my brow. "Exactly how does that apply here?"

She laughed. "You and I both know it's not over. That man wants you like a fish wants a worm."

"He dumped me."

She wiggled her head. "He got scared. You spent almost two years with him. He isn't just walking away from that."

"He already did, and even if he did try to reconcile now, it's too late."

"And my momma doesn't eat the Easter candy the minute she buys it."

"Your mom still buys Easter candy?"

"For herself."

I laughed.

"Miss Chantilly—"

"Olivia, please, drop the 'miss.' How many times are we going to have this conversation?"

"Right. Sorry, I forget sometimes. Chantilly." She stressed my name. "This isn't *Friends*. It's not going to wrap itself up in a pretty little bow for you. If you want that man, you've got to fight for him."

"Have you ever considered that maybe I don't want him anymore?" I tilted my head. "And what station is *Friends* on? I love that show."

"It's on Hulu."

"Is that one of those streaming things?"

"Don't tell me you still have cable? Dear God, you don't have a landline too, do you?"

"What if the power goes out and you can't charge your phone? How are you supposed to call 911?"

She made the sign of the cross over her chest. "Bless her, Lord."

"You're not Catholic."

"Praying for you requires an extra boost." She stood and walked to the sink. "A landline." She shook her head and laughed.

I would have felt insulted if I didn't have a valid reason for owning one. Besides, I didn't have the heart to get rid of my mom's pink princess phone. She loved that thing, and when a telemarketer called every five minutes, the ring reminded me of her.

"I just think you need to give him a chance, that's all. Poor guy's been coming by Del's every day and trying to talk to you."

"He went to Del's every day before he dumped me."

She flipped around and raised her eyebrows at me. "Oh, please. It's different and you know it."

"He had almost two years' worth of chances to figure things out. He made his decision. It's not my fault he's regretting it." I stared at my empty plate and changed the subject. "I really need to start exercising. I just gained ten pounds with one biscuit."

"You and me both."

"I'm stopping by Del's to give her my lunch order on my way to the Bennett house. You want anything?"

"A pimento and ham on rye would be great. Chips on the side. Oh, and a pickle. Obviously."

I committed the order to memory. "How many tours today?"

"Just one. A small group from Bramblett County. The woman who called was a hoot when she scheduled it. Henrietta something." She shook her head. "I can't remember her last name, but she said she wanted a haunted tour."

I groaned. "We only do those in the fall."

She fluttered her eyelashes. "But you're so good at it."

Darn it. "Fine. When are they supposed to be here?"

"Three o'clock."

"Okay. I'll do it."

She clapped her hands. "I knew it."

Thelma Sayers's Dolly Parton wig slanted to the left. As I hugged her hello, I nonchalantly knocked my head into it, hoping it would straighten.

It did.

"Chantilly, sweetie. Did you see my column today? It's a doozy!" She adjusted the wig and set it on an angle again.

I glanced at Community Café's counter and smiled at Del. She just shook her head and went through the door to the kitchen.

"I haven't had a chance yet," I said. "What's it about?"

"I heard a rumor that John Bennett fella's got a hankerin' to add an extension to his house. He wants to put a glass enclosure where the garage is and put one of those lap pools in it. Can you believe that?"

"People want what they want."

"That Yankee don't deserve living in that beautiful house if he's going to muck it up like that," Del said. She'd brought me a cup of coffee, something I'd desperately needed to gather my resolve before driving out to Bennett's house.

"Delphina Beauregard, you hush." I wiggled my finger at her. "We're a kind, gentle community. We don't spew hate like that."

"When'd that change?" A smile worked hard to break through her scowl. It won.

I shook my head. "All talk. That's what you are."

"You feel like challenging that?"

"Do it," Thelma said. "I like me a good cat fight."

We all laughed.

Thelma had been writing a weekly column for our town's newspaper since about birth. When I left for college, my momma would cut out the columns and mail them to me. I didn't have to read them because she'd fill me in on all the town gossip during our hour-long weekly calls, but I did anyway. Sweet Thelma never used a computer. She hand-wrote her columns and turned them in religiously. She's much older now, and her columns are shorter, but I don't know anyone in town who isn't excited to read them.

I gave Del our lunch orders and told her I'd be back to pick them up later. I kissed Thelma on the head and smiled at her husband behind her. He rarely left her side these days, and I worried it was because he knew something I didn't. Thelma is one of three friends who know I see ghosts, and Charlie's asked me to not say anything about his presence, so I haven't.

My best friend Gen sent me a text. I responded as I walked to my car across the street. *I'll read it later. Getting in the car.*

She'd been bugging me about reading a business proposal she and another friend put together last month. They wanted me as the third owner, but I wasn't interested. I just didn't have the heart to tell her that. I'd rather push the issue aside than tell her I didn't think anyone would want a person coming to their home to fondle them under the guise of being a professional stretcher. I didn't want to burst her bubble, but the thought of a stranger coming into my home and manipulating my body parts grossed me out. I had a feeling a lot of people would feel the same.

I shuddered at the thought. Gen recently moved to Castleberry, and I was thrilled. But she soon realized small-town life was not her thing and promptly hightailed it back to Birmingham. I missed her, but she thrived in the bigger city. Maybe I was old-fashioned? Maybe there, people thought having someone stretch your muscles while you watched *Kelly and Ryan* wasn't borderline sexual assault? Unless of course the stretcher was someone like Harrison Ford or Kevin Costner. I could get behind a business idea like that.

I drove to John Bennett's house, randomly checking my phone en route. No texts or calls from Jack, not that I was expecting any. Until the other day, he'd, as my son called it, *ghosted* me the minute he said he needed a break. In my world, ghosting is directly related to the dead, but in Austin's teenage world, it's a verb for ignoring someone.

Jack had ignored me after the initial breakup, but in the past few weeks, he'd initiated small talk at Austin's lacrosse practices, and we'd even had a brief conversation at Del's. The breakup hurt, and I wouldn't go as far as Olivia and think those few chats were his attempt to dip his toe in the water again. That pool was closed.

I groaned and tossed my phone onto the passenger seat. "You're a big girl, Chantilly. Get over it." I took five deep breaths as I pulled into John Bennett's narrow driveway, nearly filled by his large black Cadillac SUV. My car barely made it all the way in. I knew John personally because our sons played lacrosse together, but that didn't make our conversations about his home any easier.

I tapped the old lion's head door knocker and admired its echo through the large front porch. John Bennett shuffled through his foyer and greeted me with a "Great. You again."

I knew this wouldn't go well. "Good morning, John. I'm here to discuss the verandah and pool."

He pushed the door open further and stepped aside. "Come on in. Let's get it over with."

I took two steps back. "How about we start out here? With the verandah."

He stepped outside and slammed the door behind him. "Listen, I understand what the town wants, but they got to understand, I'm here because my son's here." He flung his hands around as he spoke. "You think I'd leave Massachusetts for a place like this? There isn't a good place to eat closer than Atlanta. Can't you cut me some slack? For my kid? He wants the pool."

Turner didn't strike me as the lap pool sort of kid. "John, you've got to understand. You purchased a historical property, and you signed a document saying you would honor the regulations set forth by Castleberry, Georgia, and the historical society regarding historical properties, their maintenance, and design."

"You want to know what I think of that?" He sucked in a deep breath and released it. His breath smelled like cigarettes and day-old coffee.

"Thank you, but I'm sure I have an idea." I pulled a file from my bag. "I've put together some options, but since I just recently learned about the lap pool and what I suspect is an all-season room, these will require modifications." I handed the file to him.

He flipped through the pages while shaking his head. "This isn't even close to what I'm looking for," he said as he closed the file and shoved it back to me. "Other than the verandah, everything I'm planning is going on the back of the house." He flicked his head toward the street. "No one driving by can even see back there, so I don't know why this is an issue."

"This isn't about the view from the street. It's about keeping our historical locations true to their original character, preserving them for future generations."

"That's what history books are for."

"You're from Boston, right?"

"Framingham actually, but close enough."

"Isn't that area filled with history?"

"Sure, but they don't force people to live in homes from the dark ages. They slap a sign up and they're done."

They did a lot more than that, but there was no point in arguing with him. "Do you have a copy of the blueprints? I can show them to the board. I can't guarantee they'll approve them, but it's worth a shot."

He smiled for the first time since opening the door. "Be right back." He squeezed through the door and closed it behind him. He obviously didn't want me to see anything inside, but at some point, I'd have to. People tried to sneak things past the historical society all the time, but I had my ways of getting a peek at what I needed. He handed me the blueprint tube. "Keep them. I have extras."

I drove the long way back to the historical society. I liked driving through town, and since my job included regular checks at registered historical spots, I considered it a necessity. Sometimes owners made renovations and then submitted the request after the work was finished. It's a way to manipulate the system, because once a home is changed, it's harder to change back. We can fine them and, if necessary, put liens on the property, but that's a hassle, and it never goes as planned. Usually, when someone changes something in their home, they don't have the money to make it right. The board will push back on exterior changes but usually lets the interior ones go. Those I don't see with drive-bys, but I've been known to stop and say hello for a look inside.

I drove past my favorite home in town, the old Ledbetter property. I fell in love with the place as a child, and my fascination hadn't wavered. The family who'd recently purchased the house quickly restored it to its former glory. When I saw the finished product, I cried, and I hate crying around people. But I couldn't help it. They did a fabulous job, and it brought back so many memories that the tears just flowed.

The six two-story columns surrounding the front entrance had chipped and discolored as the house sat empty, but the new repairs and a fresh coat of paint highlighted the Civil War-era home. They'd repainted the entire house white, including the side verandah, brought the faded shutters back to life with shiny black paint, and painted the ten-foot-high front door to match. Pink and white rose and azalea bushes lined the sidewalk from the driveway, which was framed with crepe myrtles in pink, purple, and white. It was stunning. Every time I drove by it, I slowed and soaked in the beauty. When the Alexander family bought the place, they asked me to help with the restoration plans so they could get it just right, and I spent weeks digging up photos from our city records. It took a lot of research here in Castleberry and in neighboring towns, but we found enough photos for them to restore it back to almost a perfect match. They'd purchased furniture that resembled the items in the photos, and had several pieces handmade to match items from the era. Mr. Alexander owned a software company in Alpharetta, Georgia, and when he sold it, he and his wife moved to Castleberry at her request. She told me she'd gone for a drive in her new convertible, found the house, and fell in love with it.

He got it for a steal too, but he'd put over five hundred thousand dollars into the restoration.

As I passed the lacrosse park, I glanced at the first field and did a double-take. An older gentleman in a blue-gray mechanic jumpsuit stood in the middle of the first field. As I passed, he disappeared into thin air.

"Here we go," I said out loud. "It's ghost time."

I did a U-turn and drove into the lot, parked my car in the closest space to the bleachers, and stared at the field. I practically jumped out of my skin when the same man appeared next to my window. Had I not seen his disappearing act before, I would have sworn he was alive. He looked that good. I rolled down my window and smiled. "Nice disappearing trick you did on the field. Was that for me?"

He stared at me but didn't speak.

"Is there, uh, something you need?"

He turned around and walked toward the bleachers.

"Am I supposed to come with you?"

He just kept walking.

"Great." I rolled up the window, shut off my car, and climbed out. "Hold on, I'm coming."

The dead didn't care about small talk or explanations. When they had a point to make, they got right to making it.

I followed him toward the bleachers. He stopped at the storage room under them. I'd been in there many times. Jack coached Austin's team and had a key, which he'd given to me to get balls or whatever he needed during practices.

The man stood next to the door silently. I stared at him. "It's locked. I don't have the key."

He glanced at the door and then focused back on me.

"Do you need something in there? I'll be back in a few hours for my son's lacrosse practice. I can get the key from the coach." I'd just have to figure out how to make that happen later.

Still no response.

"Can you tell me your name?"

Nothing.

"You're wearing a uniform. Did you work nearby?"

Nothing.

I sighed. "I'm happy to help you, sir, but you've got to work with me here. Maybe you've got an ID in those pockets?" It was a reach, but the dead surprised me all the time.

He turned back toward the locked door and disappeared.

I bent my head and shook it. "Okay then, nice chatting with you." I walked back to my car and drove straight to Community Café.

The intense Georgia heat beat down from a clear sky, and it wasn't even summer yet. Even Del's new air conditioners struggled to cool the hot air filtering in every time someone opened the door. She swiped her head with a paper towel and poured me a to-go glass of sweet iced tea. "Order's almost done. They're putting in an extra pickle for Olivia. I know how much she likes them."

"I'm sure she'll appreciate it."

"Come sit," she said, dragging me to her favorite table near the counter.

As I pulled out my chair, the café door opened. I knew the sound of the boots hitting the floor almost as well as I knew the smell of my mother's favorite perfume.

"Look who's here!" She smiled. "How's it going, Detective?" Del slid a chair from the table and angled it toward him. "Sit a spell. Your lunch'll be ready right quick." She bent toward me and whispered, "This too awkward for ya?"

I drummed my fingers on the table and whispered back, "Does that matter?"

"Not a bit."

Jack smiled at me. I smiled back. He nodded. I nodded. I waited for Del to do something, anything, even if that meant embarrassing me. I did not do awkward well at all.

"So, Austin tells me you're really running them through the ringer at lacrosse lately." I tapped my foot quietly under the table. Talking to my ex-husband Scott was easier than talking to Jack. Maybe in time that would change.

"They're doing great. We've got a good shot at winning the tournament."

Stephanie handed me my bag. "Here ya go, Miss Chantilly."

"Thanks, honey." I stood to leave. "Well, guess I'll see you at practice tonight."

He blinked. "You'll be there?"

I'd been at each practice and game, but since he dumped me, I'd kind of hidden in the shadows as much as possible. "I haven't missed one yet."

His lips parted, but he didn't say anything.

I hugged Del with my free arm and whispered, "Don't you say anything I wouldn't like, you hear?"

"I can't promise that."

Jack followed me out. "Hey, I, uh…" He shuffled his feet like a teenage boy talking to a girl for the first time.

I gave him a once-over. "New jeans?" I was completely uncomfortable, but I refused to let that show.

He glanced down, then his eyes met mine. "Yeah, how'd you know?"

Jack's eyes saw the minute details of a crime scene, but he never noticed regular things like when I got a haircut or wore a new dress. "I see a lot of things other people don't." He had no idea how true that was. I always planned to tell Jack I saw spirits when the time was right, but the time never felt right, and since he'd ended our relationship, I didn't see the need. My life was no longer his business.

Jack smiled and stepped toward me, but I backed up, staring at the older woman who had suddenly appeared behind him. I immediately recognized her from the long gray hair tied in a bun on top of her head. It was his grandmother.

She wiggled her finger at me. "He still loves you, sweetie. He just doesn't know how to say it."

I blinked when I realized Jack was speaking and I hadn't heard a word. "I'm sorry, what?"

"Where'd you go? You checked out for a second."

"Sorry, things on my mind. What did you say?"

"I was hoping you'd have time to talk after practice."

Two weeks ago I would have given my right leg for him to talk with me, but that was then. I'd moved from the hurt and desperate stage of relationship breakups to the angry stage. I didn't give even two cents about what he wanted to say. I pressed my lips together and considered my words carefully. "Thanks, but no."

His jaw dropped. "You don't want to talk or you don't have time to talk?"

I made eye contact with his grandmother.

"Go on, dear, it'll be fine."

I shrugged. "Fine. After practice."

The tension in his face disappeared. "Great. I'll see you tonight, then."

I mumbled, "Tonight, great," under my breath and hoofed it

the short distance to the historical society with Jack's grandmother on my tail. Before going inside, I stood on the front porch and talked to her with my phone to my ear in case someone walked past.

"You're his grandmother."

"Right as rain, sweetie."

"Jack doesn't know I can see ghosts."

"Oh, I know that." Her red dress hung loosely from her ghostly frame. She was tiny in life and in the afterlife, too. "He'll know soon enough, and when he's able to understand, I'll have a message for him." She smiled, and then she disappeared.

Able to understand?

CHAPTER 2

"Come on, Mom. No one else wears one."

"If your teammates played in flipflops, would you?"

Austin rolled his eyes. "That's dumb."

"So is not protecting your man parts. I want to be a grandmother someday. You're wearing a cup."

"What if I don't want kids?"

"That's irrelevant. You're my only kid, thus my only shot at a granddaughter."

"What if I marry someone who wants a boy?"

"Then you'll have to keep trying until you make me a granddaughter." I threw a pair of clean shorts at him. "Take off your shorts. They smell like rotten child."

He smiled. "I smell like roses."

"Rotting ones, maybe. Now move it, kiddo. We're running late as it is."

He dropped the dirty shorts from his waist, then stepped out of them and into the clean ones. "Are you gonna hide in the car again?"

"I'm not hiding in the car. I'm working and I don't want to be disturbed."

He used one of my "mom phrases," as he called them, against me. "Right, and I'm the tooth fairy."

Touché.

He grabbed his lacrosse bag and sat in the driver's seat while I tossed a gallon jug of water onto the floor in back.

I held the driver's side door open. "No driving today, kiddo."

"But I need forty hours to get my license."

"In nine months. I'm pretty sure we've got time to practice."

"Yeah, but only when I see Dad. You never let me drive."

I flicked my thumb toward the passenger seat. "Move it. We're going to be late."

Five minutes later we were at the park. Austin carried his lacrosse gear to the field while I hunted for the ghost I'd met earlier. He wasn't in the parking lot, but I didn't want to check the bleachers. Austin was right: I hid in the car while he practiced because I didn't want to deal with Jack. I'd changed my mind about talking the minute I said I would, and I'd come up with a million reasons I couldn't. Austin would be hungry. I had a roast in the oven. I needed to paint my toes. But the fact was, I just wasn't ready.

I stayed in the car for a bit longer, keeping an eye out for the ghost as I read through emails on my phone. Bill Chatsworth, another player's parent, pulled up beside me. He rolled down his window and smiled. I smiled back.

Bill got out of his car and walked to mine. As I rolled down my window, a blast of Georgia heat hit me.

"Everything okay, Chantilly?"

Bill's son William and Austin had been friends and lacrosse team members since we'd moved to town. William was a defense player and probably the best on the team other than Turner, John Bennett's son.

"Things are great! I'm just getting some work done before heading to watch the practice. How are you?"

"Good. I'm good." He glanced around the parking lot.

"Looking for someone?"

He blinked. "What? Oh, no. Just seeing who's here."

I nodded. Been there, done that.

Two more cars pulled up, each belonging to players' parents. Bill's eyes locked on a black SUV circling the parking lot before leaving. He quickly said goodbye and headed toward the field.

I climbed out of my car and slowly gathered my things. The longer it took, the less time I'd have to sit and stare at Jack.

A white Mercedes convertible pulled into the lot and parked a few rows away from the other cars. Travis Hendricks, Turner Bennett's stepfather, got out with a cloth in his hand and scrutinized the entire car, wiping several sections down completely. He bought the car a few weeks ago and was so anal-retentive about damaging it he refused to park near anyone.

I opened the back door and grabbed my bag. I could work on a file while sitting in the stands and feel a whole lot less awkward. When I closed the door and turned around, I noticed Travis talking to another man whose T-shirt and running shorts clung to his thin, sweaty body. He wore a baseball cap low on his forehead, and if he had hair, it was too short to see. I didn't recognize the man, so I knew he wasn't part of the lacrosse team.

A blacktop path circled the lacrosse fields, and people used it to run, walk, bike, and roller blade all the time, which I assumed was the reason for the man's clingy clothes. He was built like a runner, thin but not a lot of tone. He dragged his fingers over the Mercedes's small trunk and laughed. Travis threw his arms in the air and then rubbed the cloth over the trunk again. I laughed. Apparently, I wasn't the only one who thought he needed to chill out about the car.

The small trunk popped open, and Travis took out a golf club. He handed it to the man, who swung it like a golfer would. I knew nothing about the sport, and I had no idea Travis played.

Someone tapped me on the shoulder. Startled, I flipped

around and then relaxed when I saw Emma Henderson, a player's mom, smiling at me. "Emma! You scared me!"

She blushed. "I'm sorry. I'm just checking on you. Are you hiding out over here?"

It was my turn to blush. "Is it that obvious?"

She bit her bottom lip. "Just a little."

That did it. I finally gathered the courage to walk over to the bleachers. While Austin practiced, I sat and talked with a few of the lacrosse moms, feeling confident enough to forego hiding in my files. But when John Bennett showed up, I quickly hopped off the metal bench and headed toward the opposite side of the field. If he saw the files, he might think they were about his place, and I didn't want a confrontation. I slipped around the back of the bleachers and headed toward the storage room. Two men standing near them saw me and walked toward the parking lot.

The door to the storage area was open, so I wandered in, hoping I'd find the ghost inside. I waited a few minutes before peeking out the door, and when I didn't see anyone around, I closed it. The ghost had gone through it before, so I thought I'd have a better chance of seeing him in there if it was closed.

I was right.

As the ghost came toward me, I took two steps back and accidentally backed into the wall, knocking a team tournament photo to the ground. I picked it up and rehung it, smiling at their beaming faces. The boys worked hard, and with three new team members, they pulled off a win no one expected. It was an exciting, nail-biting final game, but it was worth it.

I turned around and smiled at the ghost, catching a glimpse of a nametag on his uniform I hadn't noticed before. "Donald Rogers. Is that you?"

Nothing. He stared at the photo.

"It's my son's team. They won first place in the tournament." As if I'd expected him to congratulate me. While he kept his eyes on the photo, I asked questions I hoped would be easily answered through his actions. "Do you have something to say about the photo?" I removed it from the wall and held it toward him. "How about the kids? Maybe my son?" I pointed to Austin, but the ghost did nothing. "This one?" I went through each child in the photo, thankful the team wasn't big, but the ghost showed no response. Frustrated, I hung it back up and tried something else. "Is there something in here? Something you need or want to show me?"

Still nothing. I moved a few boxes to the side and walked to the back. The ghost followed. Progress! He stood in front of the back wall and stared at the cleaning solutions on the shelf. His lips straightened. He blinked and then his mouth opened, but nothing came out.

I examined the items on the shelf. Just the usual things you'd find at a park: a universal cleaner, a tub of road salt, and a few things I didn't give much attention. "Is something here important to you?"

He disappeared.

"I guess not," I said. I smiled at the photo on my way out.

Turner Bennett, a new player last season, was fantastic. I'd met his mother Charlotte the first time she came to practice, but John hadn't yet moved to town. Meeting people who've divorced is interesting. I'm no relationship expert, but I could tell they weren't a match the minute I talked to John. He was boisterous and loud, and Charlotte quiet and reserved. Opposites are supposed to attract, but that doesn't promise a happily-ever-after. Then again, Scott and I were the perfect match, until he found a better perfect match. Marriage is tricky.

I didn't want to go back to the bleachers, so instead, I walked part of the path around the fields, hoping to see Mr. Rogers again. When I didn't, I headed back to the car, turned the air conditioner to high, and searched the internet for his obituary. He passed four years ago, at seventy-three, at his home in Dahlonega, Georgia.

Donald "Don" Rogers, 80, of Dahlonega passed away unexpectedly at his home Tuesday, May 12, 2016. He was born in Dahlonega on May 1, 1936. He is survived by his wife Mary (Humphrey) Rogers and son Donald Rogers, Jr. He was a maintenance and groundskeeper with the Castleberry Parks and Recreation Department for thirty years. Donations may be made to the Castleberry Parks and Recreation Department. No services planned at this time.

Unexpectedly? Was he sick? No one ever wrote the cause of death in an obituary, and though I understood why, it would make things a lot easier for psychic mediums.

An odor seeped through my car's vents. Onions. Plates and plates of onions. When teenage boys sweat, the onion smell stuck to everything in its path. I knew they were headed toward the lot without even looking.

I checked my watch and jumped out of the car. I had no idea that much time had passed. I clicked open the hatch for Austin's stinky bag and walked toward the front of the car. He jogged over, sweat dripping down his face. I easily recognized the sound of his shoes hitting the pavement.

"Mom, Coach needs to see you."

I acted surprised. "Why?"

He shrugged, tossed his bag in the car, and jogged back to the field.

I closed the hatch door and hit the lock button on my key fob, then cautiously, and as casually as I could muster, sauntered to the bleachers. I passed most of the team and their parents on the way, but a few stragglers remained.

One by one, each of them left, leaving Jack, Turner, and Austin to finish cleaning up the field. Austin bonded with Jack months before we began dating, and it was normal for him to hang around and help clean up after practice. I didn't want to change his patterns. He'd experienced enough life changes already.

They walked in my direction, but Austin and Turner kept going.

I angled my head and asked, "Hey, Turner, is your dad bringing you home?" If so, he'd left about five minutes ago without his kid.

"My stepdad's picking me up."

Jack guzzled a bottle of water. "Thanks for waiting. Is it okay to talk here?"

I stared at the ground. "I've got a call in twenty minutes." I paused to think of a reason I'd have a call planned for eight-thirty at night. "For work." I crossed my arms over my chest. "So this has to be quick."

His body was rigid, shoulders tight and back straight, but he tapped his left foot on the ground. He was as uncomfortable as I was. "I, uh, I just wanted to see how you're doing. We were friends before all this…this mess, and I was hoping maybe—"

I shoved my palm toward his face. "Wait, all this mess? You think our two years together was a mess?" I smacked my lips together and they made a popping sound. "Yeah, you're right, we were friends before all this *mess*, but that was then. Things are different now."

His eyes had been soft and kind with a hint of humility, but they hardened. I knew Jack Levitt well, and I knew those eyes, the narrowed corners of his thin lips, and his tense jaw. He was mad.

Good. Now he knew how I felt. "I have to go. See you around." See you around? What was I, twelve?

Austin and Turner stood next to my car, laughing. Austin stopped when he saw my face. "Hey," he tread carefully, his voice low and respectful. "Can Turner come hang out?"

"Not tonight, honey. It's getting late, and I've got an early day tomorrow."

He groaned. "Sorry, man."

"Dude, it's okay. My stepdad's coming to get me in a minute."

I checked the parking lot, but Travis's Mercedes wasn't there. "He was here before. Does he know he's supposed to get you?"

He shrugged. "Mom told me he was."

"Would you like us to wait with you?"

Jack walked up. "I'll hang with him," he said, looking at Turner, not me.

"Don't sweat it, Coach. He texted, said he was down the street."

Austin and I said our goodbyes, and I got us out of there as fast as I could. As I drove out of the parking lot, I noticed Mr. Rogers standing near the storage room under the bleachers again. He wanted something from me, I could feel it. I just wasn't sure what.

∼

Austin tapped on my bedroom door. "Mom, Mrs. Hendricks wants to talk to you."

I checked the digital clock on my nightstand. It was past eleven. I sat up and clicked on my table lamp. "Come on in," I said as I adjusted my nightgown. I rubbed my eyes to force them to stay open.

He handed me his cell phone. His hand trembled. "It's about Turner," he whispered.

"Hey, Charlotte, everything okay?"

Charlotte's voice shook like my son's hand. "It's Turner. I don't know where he is, and he's not answering his phone."

The urgency in her voice had me half out of bed before she finished her last sentence. "When was the last time you saw him?"

"When I dropped him off at practice."

"Okay, when Austin and I left, he was still there waiting. He said Travis was picking him up?"

"Travis? No. He never gets it right. His father was supposed to bring him home."

"I saw them both at practice, though I didn't notice either leave. But Turner said Travis texted him saying he was on his way. Are you sure plans didn't change?"

"Are you kidding? Travis and John can't stand each other. John takes every chance he gets to make Travis look bad to Turner. Pigs will fly before my ex would ask Travis for help, and that works the other way too." She blew her nose. "Besides, Travis told me he went to the field, but Turner wasn't there."

"Okay, have you called John? Maybe Turner's with him and his phone's dead."

"He's not with him. John said he had no idea he was supposed to get him. I think I should call the police."

The police. Jack. "I'll tell you what, let me call Jack. In the meantime, you call everyone on the lacrosse list. I'll have Jack get in touch with you right away, okay?"

"Thank you, I appreciate it." She sniffled. "What if something happened to him?"

"I'm sure everything's fine. Try not to worry, okay?"

"Okay."

Austin sat on the edge of my bed. "Is Turner okay?"

"Have you talked to him since practice?"

"No."

"Texted at all?"

He shook his head.

"Can you do me a favor and try texting him now?" I picked up my landline and dialed Jack's cell.

He answered on the first ring. "Hey, you okay?"

"I just spoke to Charlotte Hendricks. Turner didn't come home from lacrosse. He's not answering his cell either."

"He said his stepdad was picking him up."

"Not according to her."

"I left before anyone got him." He cursed under his breath. "What the hell was I thinking?"

"Don't. This isn't your fault. Travis said he went there, but Turner was already gone."

"Okay, let me give her a call. Thanks for letting me know."

"Can you keep me posted?"

"Sure thing."

Austin crawled onto the other side of the bed and propped himself up against the pillows. "He hasn't read my text. This is bad, isn't it?"

"Honey, has Turner ever said anything about his parents?"

He shrugged. "I don't know. Not really, I guess."

"Does he get along with his stepfather?"

"We don't really talk about it."

"What about his dad, was he happy when he moved to town?"

"We don't talk about that kind of stuff, Mom. What's going on?"

"I'm not sure." I stood and walked into my closet, pushing the door partially closed behind me. I threw on a pair of leggings and my oversized lacrosse sweatshirt, grabbed a pair of socks from the basket, and put them on under a pair of black hiking boots. I'd nail my '90s look if I still had bangs and a perm. "I'm going to run to the park right quick, okay? Can you keep your phone on in case someone calls?"

"Why?"

The person I wanted to see probably didn't care about the park's hours. "I don't know, just to look, I guess. Make sure he's not still there and hurt or something."

"Can I come?"

"No, please." He stood in front of me, his head a good four inches higher than mine. I looked up at him. "I need you to stick around here in case Turner comes by. I'm sure he's just upset about something and is blowing off steam, so you never know, he may stop by and throw rocks at your window or something."

"Why would he throw rocks at my window?"

Bless his heart, his era missed out on the best things in life. "He might come by, so just stay put, okay?"

"What should I do if he comes over or calls or something?"

"Convince him to call his mom, and then call me."

"Yes, ma'am."

I kissed his forehead. "I'll be right back."

"Okay."

∽

Our minds are much more advanced than science thinks. Sure, I've got a sixth sense now, which is pretty darn miraculous, but I'm not talking about that. I've read hundreds of articles claiming we're still connected with the people we've lost, and all we have to do is think about them and they'll be with us, whether we can see them or not.

But that's a bunch of garbage. I think about my mom and dad every single day, and you'd think, as a psychic medium, I'd see them if they were here, right? Nope. Do I get signs? Sure. But I don't generally feel them around me. I think, for the most part, when people move on, they do just that. Like I've said, the ones who stick around have reasons or just don't want to leave. When someone thinks about those spirits, the chance of them coming around is greater. Just in case, I thought about Turner, but if something had happened, he wasn't letting me in on it.

I thought about Mr. Rogers and talked to him in case he was at the park and could hear me. "I'm on my way to see you, Mr. Rogers. One of the boys from lacrosse is missing. I'm hoping you'll be able to help me figure out what's going on."

I pulled into the dark lot and dimmed my lights. If someone was there, my bright beams might scare them, and that was the last thing I wanted. I made a slow loop through the lot, but I didn't see a soul. Literally. I drove over to the bleachers and parked near the storage, then turned off the car and stepped out, using my iPhone flashlight to guide me. It was dim and barely lit up the ground below me, but it was better than nothing. A cold feeling swept through me, and I immediately felt nauseous. I froze and turned around slowly as a slimy wetness covered my skin.

I'd just walked through Mr. Rogers. "I didn't mean to do that, I can't—"

He crooked his finger, which I took to mean follow him. He walked to the storage door.

"It's locked," I said, pointing to the key padlock hanging from the bolt. "I can't get in."

He pointed to a small box behind the garbage can.

I crouched down and picked it up. "When did they change the lock?"

He smiled but didn't answer.

We stepped inside, and I clicked on the light, closing the door behind me just in case.

"Mr. Rogers, a boy is missing. Is that why we're here?"

He walked over to the team photo and pointed at it.

"Yes, he's on the team." I pointed to Turner. "Him. No one's seen him since the end of practice. Do you know what happened to him?"

He walked toward the back of the storage room again and stood staring at the wall of supplies.

I exhaled and stood next to him, staring blankly at the shelves. "Obviously, you're not a talker, but it would be a lot easier for me if you were."

He turned toward me, then back to the shelves.

"Turner was supposed to be picked up by a parent, but when I left, he was still here with the coach."

He walked back to the photo and pointed at Jack.

I nodded. "That's him." I pointed at Turner again. "They were together, but someone was supposed to pick up the boy. Maybe you saw a small white car? A Mercedes?"

He pointed at Turner, his finger almost touching the glass frame.

"Yes, him. Did you see how he left?" He didn't speak, and I tried hard to stay calm, but I just wasn't getting anywhere except frustrated. I groaned. "I can't help you if I don't understand what you're showing me."

He walked back to the shelves.

"Okay," I said, taking three large steps toward him. "The shelves it is. Let's see." I pointed to the bottom row. "Is it on here?" When he didn't respond, I moved up a level. "How about this one?" I asked about each item, but he didn't say a thing.

A siren blared, and he disappeared.

I groaned as I opened the door and saw the Castleberry police cruiser pull up next to my car. "Great," I said under my breath. "Just great."

A female officer stepped out and flashed her light at my back license plate. After two years of dating a police detective, I knew just about every officer on the department, but of course, this one didn't ring a bell. "Stop," she said.

"I am stopped. I'm Chantilly Adair. I called Detective Levitt about a possible missing boy from his lacrosse team. If you call him, he'll verify. I'm here to see if I can find the boy."

"Please step into the light with your hands out, ma'am."

I did as told. She walked over, gun drawn, with a pretty intense expression on her face. "Do you have any ID?"

"In my purse, on the passenger seat of my car."

She waved her gun at me. "In front of me, please. Lean your hands against the car."

I would never wonder what it felt like to be a criminal again.

She searched my purse and checked my ID, then stepped away and talked into the radio attached to her shoulder.

She was close enough for me to hear the woman on the other

line laugh. "You've got Ms. Adair? That's Detective Levitt's lady friend," the dispatcher said.

Not anymore, I thought.

The officer explained—in police code—what I was doing and where we were.

"Let me call Levitt. I'm sure he'll vouch for her."

Two minutes later Jack's ring erupted from my cell. "That's Detective Levitt," I said. "Should I answer?"

She nodded.

"Hey, I'm at the lacrosse park, and this nice officer is—"

"Can you put me on speaker?"

I hit the speaker button. "You're on."

"Hansen, it's Detective Levitt. A kid on my lacrosse team hasn't made it home yet. Chantilly's there having a look. Can you help her?"

"Yes, sir."

"Have you heard anything?" I asked.

"Not yet. I've spoken to his parents, but none of them can agree on what their pick-up plan was."

"Both John and Travis were there tonight."

"Bennett says he was, and Travis says he got there after practice ended, but Turner was already gone."

"That's not true. I saw him talking to some guy by his car about thirty minutes into practice."

"A team parent?"

"No. I didn't see him drive up in a car, but his clothes were sweaty so he was probably a runner or something."

"Did you see Travis leave?"

"No."

"What about Bennett?"

"Nope."

"I've got a BOLO out for him, and I'm sure he'll turn up. I'll keep you posted."

"Thanks," I said, and disconnected the call.

Officer Hansen and I checked the area around the field, but there was no sign of Turner or any of his stuff.

"I'll contact Detective Levitt, ma'am. I suggest you go home."

The ghost standing next to her beamed. She was an older woman, but not too old, maybe sixty. She smiled at me. "She can shoot better than her daddy."

I raised my eyebrows, hoping she'd get my point. "Officer, is your mother still alive?"

She narrowed her brows. "That's an odd question."

"I know. It's just that I'm a mother, and I can imagine how Mrs. Hendricks must be feeling at the moment."

"My mother died two years ago, ma'am."

"I'm sorry for your loss."

The spirit smiled. "I'm very proud of her. You tell her that, you hear?"

Oh yay! A talker. They were so few and far between. "I'm sure she was very proud of you."

"Thank you. Now I think it's best you head on home. We'll handle things from here."

"Yes, of course." I eyed the spirit and flicked my head for her to follow. As I walked to my car, she appeared next to me. I whispered, "Do you see the maintenance man? I'm trying to get him to talk to me, but he either can't or won't. Maybe you could give it a shot?"

"I'm very proud of her," she said, then disappeared.

That was probably a no.

CHAPTER 3

Austin sat at the kitchen table and stirred his Frosted Flakes around the bowl. "Turner's not answering his texts." The cereal was limp and soggy, and he'd yet to take a bite.

"I know, honey. The police are looking into what happened. I'm sure it's nothing serious."

"Did you talk to his mom again?"

Austin was asleep on the couch when I got home, so I left him there. He woke up when he heard me moving around in the kitchen hours later. "We texted late last night, but nothing since then."

"Has she heard from him?"

"Not yet. His phone is going straight to voicemail."

"What about the Find My Friends app or location services? Did she try those?"

I knew about the location services thing, but I'd never heard of the Find My Friends app. I really needed to learn more about technology. "What's Find My Friends?"

"It's a location app that shows you where your friends are. It used to be cool, but then parents found it and started spying on their kids, so we pretty much switched to Snapchat, but maybe Turner still uses it?"

A few months ago I'd read an article about iPhones and the ability to share locations through iMessage. After a thirty-minute discussion with my son, he realized he wouldn't win the argument, and we shared our locations. I didn't stalk my son—often—but I felt better knowing I could locate him if necessary. "Does Turner have an iPhone?"

He nodded.

"I'll ask his mom about the location services and the friends thing. Can you check and see if you can find him on your Snap?"

He scrolled through his phone. "Last update was at the lax park."

"After practice?"

He shook his head. "Right when we started."

"Honey, are you sure he's never said anything about his parents?"

"We don't talk about that stuff."

"What do you talk about?"

"I don't know, lacrosse, video games."

"Girls?"

"The girls around here are gross."

"Nice." I tried to lighten the mood. Austin didn't need to carry that worry around with him.

"Are the police looking for him?"

My cell rang and Charlotte's ID popped onto the screen. "Hey, Charlotte. Any news?"

"No, but Amy Ashford is setting up a search party for the park and the surrounding area. She's calling all the lax parents, but I told her I'd call you. I spoke to Coach Levitt, and the police are going to participate. He told me I have to stay home in case Turner calls. I'm just so upset." She sniffled. "I can't stay home, but if I leave and he calls the landline or comes home, I could miss it."

"No, Charlotte, you definitely should stay home. What time is the search? Austin and I will be there."

"The police are already there. It's supposed to start at nine o'clock."

"Okay, listen, you've got my cell. If you hear anything, you call Jack first, but make sure to call or text me. I'll make sure word gets out if you want something known."

"Thank you, Chantilly, so much. I'm so glad you're here. I can't imagine doing this all alone."

"You're not alone. You'll have the entire town out looking for Turner at nine, I promise."

And I was right.

Even Thelma and Del came to help. They weren't up to hiking in the woods surrounding the lacrosse field, but Del set up a water and coffee station and the two handed out cups, creamers, sugars, and cups of water for free. I'd called Olivia and she showed up to help with the search.

Amy printed copies of Turner's most recent photo and handed them out to volunteers. We had over two hundred people searching for Turner or a sign of him, and after six hours and still no sign, Jack called everyone in.

"Why's he stopping?" Thelma asked.

"I think we've searched all of Castleberry twice over. Maybe he wants to give everyone a break?"

"But what if that poor child needs help? What if he's hurt, or unconscious, and he can't walk?" Thelma's bottom lip quivered. "This is just awful."

She bent her head and cried into her hands, and her Dolly Parton wig shifted a little to the right. As I hugged her, I adjusted it with a push of my head.

"They'll find the boy, Thelma. Don't you worry. Castleberry people don't go missing for long. Boy's probably out messing around, not paying attention to the clock." Del patted Thelma on the back. "You just watch. He'll show up."

Del's heart was in the right place, but it had been nearly twenty-four hours and nothing. No calls, no texts, no locating apps, no social media updates, nothing.

As I walked toward my car, I noticed Mr. Rogers over by the storage room again. I wandered over, being as inconspicuous as possible in case anyone was watching.

"How's it going?" I asked.

He smiled.

The storage room door was open, and I followed him in. I looked behind me and closed it when I saw no one looking. I squinted when I flipped on the overhead light.

Mr. Rogers stood beside me, his smile never changing.

I tried to stay calm and patient, but when he pointed at the team photo and then walked over to the shelves again, I wanted to scream. I squeezed my hands into fists. "Yes, the team photo, the shelves. We've been through this. I can't help you if you can't communicate with words. I don't know what else to tell you."

His eyes darkened. I stepped back. A ghost was one thing, but a mad ghost? That scared me.

He stepped closer and, in a barely audible voice, said, "Please, help me."

My eyes widened. "I...I...okay. I'm trying."

He pointed to the shelves, and all of a sudden, the room closed in on me. The walls, the shelves, it all crowded me, making me claustrophobic. My lungs tightened, and I gasped for breath. I stared at him and his smile disappeared. I coughed and pressed my hand into my chest. "I...I can't..." I couldn't get the words out. I ran to the door and pushed it open, then rushed out into the fresh air, gasping for breath. I practically fell into Jack.

"Hey, you okay?"

"I...I..." I took a deep breath and slowly released it. "I'm... yeah, I just...I'm fine." I moved away from his grasp and gazed into the storage room. Mr. Rogers was gone. "I was just checking in there." I closed the door. "Did you know they changed the lock? It's a padlock now instead of the door lock. And they hid the key in a box." I crouched down to grab the box, but it was gone. "Huh. It's gone now, but I used it last night."

He shifted to the side and examined the doorknob. "Looks like the regular lock to me."

Either the ghost showed me what he wanted me to see, or he somehow finagled a different lock, granting me access to the room. I made a mental note to pay better attention.

Jack just stood there like he wanted to say something, or maybe wanted me to say something.

I tend to talk when I'm nervous or uncomfortable, and I was a whole lot of both. "Hey," I said. "Did you know Donald Rogers?"

"Big Don or his son?"

"The one who worked for the park."

"Big Don. Everyone knew him. Why?"

Everyone but me. "Someone mentioned his name on the search," I lied.

"He was a nice guy. I think almost every city employee went to his funeral."

"Do you know how he died?"

"Not the details, just that it was sudden. Why are you asking about Big Don?"

"They said he'd know where to look for a kid who didn't want to be found."

He smiled. "Don worked for the city forever. He knew the parks well."

"Too bad he's not around to help then."

The chief of police, Steve Hagarty, walked over. Jack's entire demeanor changed from casual to professional. "Chief."

"Detective." He smiled at me. "Ms. Adair."

"Chief Hagarty." I nodded once. "How's Alice?"

Steve Hagarty had been Castleberry's police chief for thirty years. He was set to retire in December, but according to Jack, he mentally retired months ago. He *phoned it in*, Jack said, but the department ran itself. If anything could bring the chief back into the game, it would be a missing child. Back in the late '80s, his son, Steve Junior, was found dead on Highway 53 outside of Jasper. Everyone except Alice thought he'd run away. He and his dad didn't get along, and the rumor was they'd had a fight and the boy left. Sadly, that wasn't the case. Steve Junior had hitched a ride on the highway and drew the death card. They never caught the killer, but the police believed it was the same person who killed three other young men across the South that year.

Steve Junior had appeared to me several times, but he'd never once asked me to deliver a message or said he needed help, so I just let him be.

The chief put his heart and soul into finding his boy, and when he couldn't, he threw himself even more into work. My mother once told me it broke Alice's heart to lose both her son and her husband at the hands of a murderer.

"Alice is good, thanks for asking." He redirected his attention to Jack. "Any word on the boy?"

Jack shook his head. "I've called off the search for now. We've checked a two-mile perimeter around the park. The BOLO's out and a group is distributing flyers. I'm heading to talk with the parents again."

"Hold up on that, okay? I'd like to have Officer Hansen talk to the parents."

Jack's eyebrow rose. "Yes, sir, but I've already—"

Steve nodded. "I know, son, but we've got a bit of a problem."

Jack's jaw hardened.

"If you'll excuse me," I said. "Chief Hagarty, I hope you all can find the boy quickly."

I helped Del and Thelma finish packing up the coffee and water and carried everything to Del's car.

Thelma climbed into the passenger seat and groaned. "Lordy be, I am give slap out. Who knew all this searching could be so hard?"

"Searching? How's sitting on your butt handing out water searching?"

"I'm here at the search, so it counts. Besides, my legs can't handle that amount of walking no more. They hurt like the dickens."

"I feel your pain," I said, and meant it. My sciatic nerve throbbed something fierce. I should go home and ice it, but I knew I wouldn't.

Jack leaned against my car with his head down.

"Hey, you okay?"

"Got a minute?"

His tired eyes and heavy sigh told me it was important. "Sure. What's up?"

"I'm off the case."

"The case? You mean Turner?"

He nodded.

"What? Why?"

"Persons of interest don't investigate crimes."

"Persons of interest?" I shook my head. "No. The chief can't think that."

"He doesn't, but it's procedure. As far as he knows, I was the last one with Turner."

"You did not do anything to that boy."

"Chief knows that, but he can't keep me on the case."

I ran my hand through my hair. "I can't believe this is happening to you. What can I do to help?"

"Hansen's the lead. If she comes to you about last night, just tell her the truth."

"I'll tell her you didn't do anything. That's the truth."

He tried to smile, but he couldn't pull it off. "Just promise me you won't let your feelings for me impact how you answer her questions."

"Which feelings? My recent ones or the ones from a few weeks ago?"

A smile crept across his face. "Both."

Austin and the rest of the lacrosse team decided to do their own search for Turner. The boys were all pretty close and thought going out to their favorite places might help. If nothing, Austin hoped their tour of town would jar one of them into remembering something Turner said. I hoped he was right. I knew searching was important to him, but I couldn't focus while he was gone. I took a shower, changed my sheets, changed his sheets—how could one teenager make sheets smell so awful—and dusted the entire house. Until he got home, I'd just stay a hot mess of nerves praying nothing happened to him.

I opened my front door to Officer Hansen's stern, thin-lipped expression. She was in uniform, but her brown hair was in a ponytail instead of the bun from last night.

"Ms. Adair, remember me?"

"Of course, Officer Hansen, right?"

"Yes, ma'am. I'm working the missing child case, and I have a few questions for you."

"Come on in."

She took a few steps in and examined my home. "Nice place. You do the updates yourself?"

Nice cop, that's what she wanted to play? Okay, I could work with nice cop. "I picked everything out, but no, I didn't do the work. I don't have that kind of talent."

"You've got great taste, though."

"Thank you."

We wandered to the kitchen, where I pointed to the table. "Have a seat. Would you like something to drink?"

"No, ma'am. Thank you. And I prefer to stand."

"Suit yourself. Any news?"

"One of the searchers found a cloth at the far end of the woods near the lacrosse park."

"A cloth?"

"Yes, ma'am."

"And you think it has something to do with Turner?"

"We can't say for sure, ma'am."

"A lot of people hang out in those woods."

"We're aware of that."

"I guess it's better than nothing."

She nodded. "I understand you were one of the last parents at the park? Can you tell me what happened?"

Jack wanted to talk about our relationship, and I didn't want to? Probably not what I needed to say. "Sure. Jack and I were talking. Austin—that's my son—and Turner were over by my car. Austin asked if Turner could come over, but I said no. In retrospect, I should have said yes. Jack stayed with Turner, who was waiting for a parent to pick him up."

"Do you know which parent?"

"He said his stepdad, Travis."

"Did you see Mr. Hendricks arrive?"

"He was there earlier, but I think he left. John Bennett was there too, but again, I think he left."

"Mr. Bennett was at the park?"

"Yes."

"Did you talk to him?"

"No."

"But you're sure it was him?"

"Yes. Mr. Bennett is trying to make some changes to his home, and as the historical society manager, I've had to meet with him several times."

"Can you tell me what kind of vehicle Mr. Bennett drives?"

"It's a Cadillac SUV, black."

She nodded as she took down notes. "What about Mr. Hendricks?"

"A Mercedes convertible."

She nodded. "Did Detective Levitt say anything to you about the boy?"

"Like what?"

"You tell me."

"No. Detective Levitt didn't say anything about the boy."

"What were you two discussing?"

"We were having a private conversation that has nothing to do with Turner's disappearance."

"About?"

"Something private."

"Did it have anything to do with the team?"

"Officer Hansen, Detective Levitt is an excellent coach and an honest, good man. He did nothing to Turner Bennett."

"Did he get into his vehicle when you did?"

"No."

"Did he say he'd take Turner home?"

"No. He said he'd wait with him, which he usually does with whichever kid is last to get picked up."

She pressed her lips together and nodded as she jotted that down. "What's Turner's relationship with the coach like?"

"I think that's something you should ask the *coach*."

She glanced up from her notepad again. "Did you ever see them in a tense situation? Detective Levitt yelling at him or pulling him aside maybe?"

"Jack only yells at the kids when they're on the field, and that's so they can hear him. He's not yelling at them in an angry way."

"And off the field?"

"As I just said, no." She wanted to trap me, but I wasn't falling for it. "Officer Hansen, Jack Levitt is an excellent coach. He's very supportive of the players and has positive relationships with them. Why do you think the team is so good? It's not just the players that make a team, you know.

And you can ask any of the kids, they'll tell you they adore Jack."

"I understand you two dated?"

"Does that matter?"

"You could be protecting him."

I poured myself a glass of water, but I didn't offer Officer Hansen any. "Jack's a police detective. He's one of the good guys, not a kidnapper."

She didn't bother responding. "Have you spent any time talking with Turner Bennett?"

"Not about anything personal. I've asked my son if he's said anything about his parents, but Austin said no. You're welcome to talk with him, though."

"Is he home?"

"No. The team is out searching for their friend."

"Do you know where they went?"

"I can text him if you'd like."

"No, thank you. I'll be talking with all of them."

"Officer Hansen, may I make a suggestion?"

She kept her pencil in hand but stopped writing.

"I don't know what's going on with the parents, but Charlotte mentioned that John and Travis don't get along. It's my experience that divorce is hard on a kid. Maybe that's caused some issues for Turner."

"We're looking into it."

"Good, then you'll realize Jack has nothing to do with this."

"I'm just doing my job, ma'am."

"Noted." I'd been leaning against my kitchen counter and pushed myself off. "If there's nothing else, then…"

She flipped her notepad closed and stuffed it in her pocket. "If you hear anything or think of anything else, please contact me." She handed me a card.

"Of course," I said, walking her back to the front door.

I closed the door behind her and backed up against it. "Great."

I took a deep breath, held it for a second, and then released it as I rolled my shoulders forward. Tension rolled off me, and I relaxed. I took a seat on the new leather couch in the den and stared blankly at the dark TV screen.

I am a firm believer that everything happens for a reason, and there are no coincidences in life. I believe ghosts come to me for a reason, that I was chosen to help them. I don't know much about spirits. I don't meditate, or burn sage, or go to haunted houses, or read Tarot cards. I just talk to dead people and do my best to help them. So I know that Mr. Rogers appeared to me for a reason, and based on my previous experiences, that reason was somehow connected to Turner's disappearance. I either needed to find the boy to help the spirit, or help the spirit to find the boy.

Since Mr. Rogers appeared to me before Turner's disappearance, I believed the key to both started with him. I searched online through our community paper's articles, then checked through the *Dahlonega Nugget's* archived articles. I read quotes from friends, family, and co-workers about his passing as well as his time with Castleberry's parks and recreation department.

One quote from Mr. Rogers's son got me thinking. It wasn't what he said, but the inflection I tagged onto it. The emotion in his words seemed obvious to me. "At least he won't be harassed anymore," he said. I opened a new tab and searched for home addresses for both Don and his son. Mrs. Rogers still lived in Dahlonega, but there were five current addresses listed for their son.

"You're going to wear out my new wood floors pacing like that. Sit your butt down, please."

He dropped into a kitchen chair and muttered under his breath.

Normally he'd get a switch to his behind for that kind of talk, but given the circumstances, I let it go.

"Coach wouldn't hurt any of us." He slid the side of his hand under his nose. "No way."

I ripped a paper towel from the roll and handed it to him. "The chief knows that."

"Coach is like, the best, Mom. He's nicer than most dads I know."

"I know." I stretched up onto my tiptoes and removed a large plastic cup from the top cabinet and filled it with ice. "Officer Hansen is going to talk to all y'all. When she does, just tell her the truth, but tell her that too."

"She talked to us already, and we all told her that. We said no way would he do anything to one of us."

The officer worked fast. She'd just left me a little over an hour ago. I was surprised she found them so quickly. I filled the glass with water and handed it to him. "Drink this and then you need to get some sleep. It's late."

He downed the glass of water in a few big gulps and then rolled his eyes. "I'm not a kid anymore."

I took the glass from him, pinched the sleeve of his discolored beige T-shirt between my thumb and forefinger, and yanked him toward his room. "You'll always be a kid to me, so get used to it."

He dragged his feet and whined the whole way to his room. But his tone changed as he pulled off his shirt. "What's going to happen?"

"I don't know, but I know they'll find a way to clear Jack and let him find Turner. He's a good detective. He'll find him."

"What if it's too late?"

My poor child. His only experiences with death were my mom and dad, and though he was old enough to feel the pain, he was also young enough to detach from it shortly after. Losing someone his age would be an emotional knockout for him, something that could change his life forever, something he'd never forget. "Honey, they'll do their best. That's all I can tell you."

"I know."

I didn't exactly tuck him in. He refused to let me, but I did get to kiss him on the forehead. It wasn't much compared to his younger years, but I took it as a win. I missed my times with the younger boy, and knowing these years would fly by just as fast as those did, I didn't miss any opportunities.

Even though he was safe and sound at home, I still struggled to relax. Sleep seemed impossible, so I finally gave up and climbed out of bed. I checked under Austin's door and saw the dull glow of his cell phone light shut off. I shuffled around the house trying to connect Mr. Rogers and Turner, but other than the lacrosse park, I couldn't.

When I finally did get to sleep, it came in fits, with bits and pieces of nightmares flickering through my head like movies on a reel. A dream of Turner Bennett lying in a ditch on the side of the road woke me. I was sweaty and breathless, and I couldn't help but think it was more than just a dream.

CHAPTER 4

I sat at my desk at the historical society office and shook my head, blushing with embarrassment. "I can't believe I did that."

"Don't worry about it. They rescheduled anyway."

"Before I stood them up or after?"

"Before." She tried not to smile, but she did anyway.

"Thanks for telling me!"

She laughed. "Honestly, with everything that's been happening, I totally forgot." She smiled bigger. "But it sure was fun watching you get all worked up about blowing off a haunted town tour."

"Did they reschedule?" Say they didn't, I thought. Please, say they didn't.

"They're calling again. One of the women has a bunion and it is, I quote, 'yanking my chain somethin' fierce.' She also said one of her man toys has to take her to the doctor for it." She exaggerated her already strong Southern accent for the quote.

"Man toys?"

"It must be an old lady thing. My grandmother says that every time she goes on a date."

"How many dates does she go on?"

"Let's see." She tapped her finger on her chin. "Last weekend, three, I think."

"Uh. Wow."

"I guess there are a lot of single men in her age group."

"Where does she find them?"

"You're not going to believe this. Senior centers. They're like clubs for old people."

"I'm familiar with them," I said, smirking at her surprise.

"Her favorite is the one in Cumming. She told me it's next to the library and a lot of couples sneak out and"—her body trembled—"smooch in the library aisles."

I cringed. "Oh."

"It's gross, but that's not even the worst of it."

"I'm afraid to ask."

"It's just that here I am. I'm single and in the prime of my life, and I'm good on the eyes, but I can't find a decent guy anywhere."

I bit my bottom lip. "Karma?"

Her eyes widened. "For what?"

"Making me feel awful for missing a tour that was already canceled?"

We both had a good laugh.

She removed the tea bag from her cup. "The bunion issue was such an overshare."

I smirked. "Have you ever had a bunion?"

"No, but I looked them up online. The photos were disgusting."

"They don't feel all that great either."

"Ew."

I laughed. "What's the plan for today? Any tours?"

She shook her head and sipped her tea. "But you do have a message on our general voicemail from Mr. Bennett."

"I'm assuming he's putting a hold on the redesign?"

She shook her head. "Nope."

"Seriously?"

"He said the crew is coming to start the verandah this morning." She glanced at the clock. "In five minutes."

I pushed back from my desk and sighed. "His kid is missing and he's having his home remodeled. Who does that?"

"Mr. Bennett."

"It's wrong."

"My grandma always says men are like bras. You never know what's inside them until you get them naked."

I almost spit out my own drink. "What does that have to do with John Bennett's verandah?"

"Nothing, but it's funny."

"Your grandmother seeing naked men is funny?"

She grimaced. "Ew. No. I didn't think about it like that."

I tossed my laptop back in my briefcase and waved as I walked out of my office. I unconsciously slowed at the stairs. I'm more careful since my fall. Olivia thinks I'm afraid I'll fall again, and I am, but I'm more afraid I'll lose my gift, or worse, gain one I couldn't handle.

Turner's face was all over town. The volunteers did a great job making sure everyone saw his face enough times to commit it to memory. They taped flyers to signs, doors, and windows, and several people were still handing them out on the street. Castleberry's not a big town, and everyone already knew Turner disappeared, but people wanted to help any way they could.

A drive down the town's main strip looked like a slideshow of Turner's picture, and my eyes welled with tears when I saw the large signs saying *Praying for Turner* hanging across storefront windows.

Olivia promised to handle the office load, even offering to go over the redesign for another historical home recently purchased by an out-of-state couple. She wasn't quite up to speed on reading blueprints, but if she took her time, she would eventually figure them out. I told her I'd be back as soon as possible, but from the looks of the trucks and building materials in Bennett's yard, I wasn't sure when that would be.

I walked over to John Bennett and the construction crew talking with him. "John, a word, please?"

"Just a sec."

No "hello," no "nice to see you," and no "have they found my son." I liked the man less and less, and I didn't really like him much in the first place.

"Gentlemen." I spoke over John Bennett. "I'm sorry, I'm going to need you to stop the project. Mr. Bennett here doesn't have the historical society's approval to make any changes on his home."

One of the crewmen glanced at me. "It's a historical home?"

I held up the file. "I have the paperwork right here. His application for changes was denied, but we were in the process of trying to come to an agreement. 'In the process' being the key to that sentence." I stuffed the file under my arm and stuck out my hand. "Chantilly Adair, Castleberry's historical society director. And you are?" I gripped his hand and rotated mine to the left. My dad once told me real men shook that way, and I'd done so ever since. Sometimes it intimidated men and sometimes it impressed them. This guy was the latter.

"Bubba Hudson. My apologies, we weren't aware of the historical significance of the home, ma'am."

"I assumed as much. Owners can't make exterior changes to any historical property here without written consent from City Council and the Historical Architectural Review Board, and we haven't given that approval."

John Bennett grunted. "It's my house, I can do what I want to it."

"You signed a contract stating any exterior and potential interior changes would be brought to the board for approval."

"And I did that."

"And those changes were denied."

He waved his hand dismissively. "I did what was required of me."

"Gentlemen, if you'll excuse us for a moment." I didn't want to push, but I also didn't want to embarrass him in front of the men.

Bubba whistled loudly and told the crew to start packing up.

John grunted and barked at me, "If I have to pay for today, I'm sending a bill to the city."

I nodded and offered him a compassionate, sincere smile. "Feel free. How are you?"

His mouth twitched and he stared at the ground. "Just trying to keep busy. Police won't let me do anything. Said I got to stay home in case he comes back."

"I'm sorry you're going through this."

"Brought the construction crew here to start so I could keep my mind off it, but you got to come and screw it up."

"If we can come to an agreement on the changes, and they have the necessary permits, they can start. I'm not sure how you got them here today without any permits as it is."

He didn't respond.

"Please, just take a look at my ideas. I think you'll be pleased."

"They aren't going to find him. Turner's gone."

My eyes widened. "They will. Our department is small, but they're good. They'll find your son."

Tears filled his eyes. He quickly wiped them away and turned so I couldn't see his face. "I'll look at the plans, but I don't see me changing my decision. If I can't get this crew back, I'll just pay another one to do it. Anyone can be bought."

I hung back while the crew reloaded their trucks. When John Bennett went inside, I walked over to Bubba. "You can lose your business license for working without a permit. You know that, right?"

He set a large saw in the back of his truck and blushed. "Yes, ma'am, but my cousin works at the county clerk's office, and she knows someone in the city clerk's office, so I usually get a pass."

I committed the name of his company to memory. "Interesting."

"And he just hired us yesterday. Said he wanted to get started right away."

"His son went missing recently. I'm sure he's trying to keep busy."

"It's his boy? The one whose picture's all over town?"

"Yes. His name is Turner Bennett."

"Man, that's too bad. I feel for the guy. They know what happened yet?"

I shook my head.

"I'll tell my crew to be on the lookout. And I'll give Mr. Bennett a call in a few days about the work."

The men left as I knocked on John Bennett's door.

It whipped open. He scowled when he saw me. "What? They're gone, and I got stuff to do."

"This will just take a minute. It's about your son."

His face softened.

"May I come in?"

He pushed the door open all the way. "Why not?"

We stood in the front foyer of the small home. He studied me carefully. Why, I wasn't sure.

I took a deep breath and cut him some slack. "Divorce is hard on kids. When my husband and I went through it, my son struggled. He became closed off, buried himself in video games—though that's not changed much—and didn't want to talk to his dad for a long time. I'm not sure what's going on with Turner, but I thought we could talk. We might think of something that can help the police."

"What's talking about my personal life with you gonna do for the cops?"

I shrugged. "Like I said, Austin didn't want to talk to his dad when we split up. We moved here, but Scott stayed in Birmingham. His relationship with his dad suffered because of it."

"Husband cheated, eh?"

I kept my expression stoic. "He found someone else, yes."

He nodded. "Me and my son are fine. It's Hendricks he's got the problem with. He doesn't like that piece of crap, and neither do I. Way he treats my kid? That's why I moved here. And now this? Cops got to know it's because of him. Turner's a good boy. He wouldn't run away like this without reason. Hendricks did something to him."

"Have you told any of this to Officer Hansen?"

He nodded. "Every word."

"What did she say?"

"Said his mom and that piece of—" He stopped and took a breath. "She and Hendricks both said everything was good between them. I told the cops that's a lie, but I don't know if they believed me."

"What makes you think Travis would want to hurt your son?"

"He doesn't love Charlotte, and he sure as heck doesn't love my kid. I see how he looks at them when he thinks no one's watching."

He was desperate and upset, but I'd seen the way Travis looked at his wife. I didn't think he could hurt her that way. "The police are talking to everyone. They'll find him, John."

His eyes narrowed. "The lady cop was asking all kinds of questions about your boyfriend. Said he's the last person to see my kid. I told her Turner likes Coach, but that doesn't mean he wouldn't hurt my kid." He used two fingers and pointed at his eyes. "You tell him I'm watching him."

I didn't bother defending Jack. Bennett wouldn't believe me anyway.

He opened the front door. "Just get me those approvals. Turner wants to move in with me, and I want it done quick."

I used my GPS to direct me to Mr. Rogers's house in Dahlonega and parked in front. The small white home was nice but it needed some work. White paint peeled off the siding and rain had done a number on the roof.

Shuffling feet echoed from the other side of the door, reminding me of a younger Austin. I used to get on him for dragging his feet when he walked. The additional effort to lift each foot off the ground was a lot of work, he said, and he was just too tired. Funny, he only walked that way when he was doing something he didn't want to do or going somewhere he didn't want to go.

Mrs. Rogers opened the door, and I understood the reason for the shuffling. "Yes?" Her voice trembled as she spoke, and her shaking hands couldn't keep the door still. She was fragile and thin, and probably weighed all of eighty pounds soaking wet, and most of her varying shades of gray hair was wrapped up in a bun. I hoped to have half that hair at her age. But her body? The signs of betrayal were clear. Mrs. Rogers had Parkinson's.

"Mrs. Rogers? My name is Chantilly Adair." She squinted and took a step closer. I hooked my purse over my shoulder in case I needed both hands to help her.

She touched her bun. "What happened to Shelly?"

"Shelly?"

"She's the girl who usually does my hair. Why isn't she here?"

"Oh, no, ma'am. I'm not a stylist." I touched my disheveled mop. "I'm sure that's obvious from my messy hair."

"God bless you for that. It thins as we age. I don't have half the hair I had back in the day."

Considering her hair was twice as thick as mine, my hair's future looked dim, but I smiled. "My name is Chantilly Adair. I work for the historical society in Castleberry."

She tilted her head. "The historical society in Castleberry?

Don't know why you'd be all the way out here, but what can I do for you?"

I shifted my weight to my left side. "I'm not here about the historical society. I'm here about your husband. I was hoping we could talk?"

Her eyes widened. "About my Don? Okay. You can come in, but please excuse the mess," she said as she shuffled into her small living room. "I don't get around too easy anymore, and I just can't keep up. My son comes by once a week, but boys don't know how to clean like us women. I'm just grateful for the help."

I sat on her couch. "Your home is lovely."

She sat on the chair across from me. It was so old and the color pattern so worn I wasn't sure if it was originally white or cream. "Well, thank you. That makes me feel better. I used to take great pride in this place, but I just can't do it with my condition." She placed her hands on her lap. "Now what is it you'd like to know about my Don? God rest his soul."

Poor Mr. Rogers didn't seem to be resting a whole lot lately.

Telling someone their dead loved one is still around is tricky, and that's why I try not to do it. Since I started seeing spirits, I've only relayed messages a handful of times, and none of them turned out remotely close to what I'd planned. My friend Angela does it all the time and says it gets a lot easier, but I'm not comfortable with it just yet. Mr. Rogers wasn't in the room with us, so if he did have a message, he wasn't ready for me to deliver it.

"One of the boys on my son's team is missing. I did some research on the park, and I found some articles about your husband's passing. I spoke to the chief of police, and he told me your husband had some trouble at the park. I'm not sure if there's a connection, but I was hoping we could talk about what happened."

"Don had a time of it the few months before he passed. He said some men were trying to steal from the teams. I told him not to get involved, but my husband didn't like seeing injustice, and he said something to those men. They got on him, telling him to mind his own business. When he told me they threatened him, I told him to go to the police. He did, but there wasn't much they could do about it, I guess."

"Did he tell you what he thought they were trying to steal from the teams?"

"Maybe something about their players or their plays?" She glanced down at her lap. "I'm sorry. I've never much understood sports."

I smiled. "I've watched football since I was a kid, and I still can't tell you anything about how it's played."

She laughed. "I always told Don it was just a bunch of men chasing a ball, but he told me the kids at the park weren't playing football. I can't recall what it was, though."

"Lacrosse. My son plays. Mrs. Rogers, your son was quoted in one of the articles. Was he referring to the problems at the park?"

She nodded. "He thought the police should have done more to help his pa. Thought his passing was because of those men harassing him. He got on the chief about it, but there wasn't much they could do then."

I considered my next question carefully. "Do you think the situation led to your husband's passing?"

She took a deep breath and let it out before speaking. "Don always had battles at work. If it wasn't one of the workers, it was one of the parents. I was always telling him to leave his work at the parks, but he never could do that. All that stress? It can damage the body."

"Did your husband ever mention any names?"

She sighed. "Not that I remember."

"Could he have mentioned any to your son?"

"He could have. My Donny, I worry about him. He's still sour about his pa's passing. I keep telling him the stress is what took his pa. I can't afford to lose him too. My heart couldn't take it."

"I completely understand."

"You think this has something to do with the missing boy?"

"I'm not sure, but I'd like to talk to your son. Would you mind giving me his number?"

She used the chair arms to angle herself and opened the drawer of the side table next to her. It took her a minute to write down the information. "Can you read this? My hands tremble so much, sometimes I can't even read my own writing."

I read the numbers to her.

She nodded. "When you talk to him, let him know you talked to me. His temper heats up quick when people talk about his pa."

"Of course." I stood. "Thank you for talking to me. You've been very helpful."

"If you think the men who harassed my Don have something to do with the missing boy, you make sure the police know, you hear? Don would want that."

I stopped at the lacrosse park on my way back to the historical society. I parked next to the bleachers and walked over to the storage room, tucking my key fob and cell phone in my pants pocket. I smiled when I saw the padlock and key box on the ground. My ghost buddy had struck again. I unlocked the door and opened it, but I waited outside, hoping Mr. Rogers would show up.

When he did, I walked inside the storage room and toward the back wall. He followed.

"Mr. Rogers, your wife is lovely."

He smiled.

"She told me you were really upset about the men at the park. She said you thought they were trying to steal from the team, and when you confronted them, they started harassing you."

His smile faded.

"Mr. Rogers, I want to help you, and I know you want to help me, but we don't have a lot of time. Are the men who harassed you the same men who took Turner Bennett?"

Jack's text sound chimed loudly from my hand. Mr. Rogers's eyes widened, and he disappeared.

"Darn it!" I read Jack's message. *They're bringing me in for questioning. Standard procedure.*

They're arresting you? The little blue dots on my phone frustrated me. Text faster, I thought.

He responded, *Just talk.*

I stuffed my phone into my pocket and walked out of the storage room, jumping back when the ghost appeared. "Oh heavens, that still scares me when y'all do that." I patted down the wrinkles in my shirt. "That was the coach. He's being brought in for questioning. Mr. Rogers, he didn't do anything to Turner. You know that, don't you? Please, help me find the boy."

He walked to the back shelves again and studied them carefully.

I examined everything on them, and I still had no clue what he was trying to tell me. "What're you trying to show me?"

He moved to the far end of the shelves. I followed, eyeing everything carefully. I moved the items on the center shelf around to see what was behind them. A small container was buried in the back against the wall. I pointed to it. "Rat poison? Is this why we're here?"

He focused on the container, but he still didn't speak. After a minute, he left the storage room and walked into the parking lot, then turned around and crooked his finger for me to follow. Instead of walking the entire way, he'd fade away, then appear a few feet from me, then disappear and do the same thing over again.

By the time we got to the woods at the opposite end of the park, I'd walked a good quarter of a mile. I was not wearing the right shoes for that.

He gazed into the woods and then at me, but he still wouldn't talk.

I ran my hand through my hair. "Did the park have rats?" I shivered at the thought. "Were they coming in from the woods?"

He turned around and headed back to the storage room.

I held my hands out in front of me. "I don't know what we just did here, but okay."

He stood by the fence surrounding the playing field.

I leaned against it and stared at the empty field, trying to connect the dots. The obvious answer is usually the right one, but that's not always the case with ghosts. "The poison. It's connected to both you and the missing boy, isn't it?"

He walked through the fence and into the playing field, then disappeared.

"Well," I mumbled under my breath, "so much for a definitive answer."

As I headed back to my car, I made a quick check in the storage room again. I took photos of the rat poison and then carefully moved everything back in front of it. When I closed the door, the padlock and hook were gone. In their place was a regular key deadbolt lock. I glanced down at the ground and saw the box for the key was gone too. I realized then that every time I used Jack's key to the storage room, it was for a deadbolt, not a padlock. Best I could figure was that when Mr. Rogers was alive, the door had a padlock, and since his passing, it was changed. I shook my head. "Um, Mr. Rogers? I can't lock the door." He wasn't around, but that didn't mean he couldn't hear me. I waited a minute, but he didn't return. "Okay, well, I guess it's just going to stay like this." I tried to wiggle the handle, but the door was locked. "Thanks," I said. I noticed chips on the door frame near the lock. Someone had tried to get in. I snapped photos of it just in case.

Then I drove to the police department to check on Jack.

The officer behind the glass partition recognized me. "I'm sorry, Ms. Adair, Detective Levitt is detained at the moment."

"I'm assuming you mean that literally."

He gave me a deadpan stare.

"I'm here to see Chief Hagarty anyway."

He smiled with relief, like I'd just taken a heavy box from him. "One sec."

Five minutes later, after I'd practically paced a hole in the floor, the chief's assistant came for me. "This way, Ms. Adair."

Chief Hagarty stood from behind his desk as I walked into his small office. "Ms. Adair, pleasure to see you." He held out a hand toward the chair. "Please, have a seat. You're here about Jack, correct?"

"Actually, no. I'm here about Donald Rogers."

His right brow went up. "Don? From parks and rec? That Don?"

I nodded.

He sat back down. "He's been gone for what, five years or so?"

"Four."

"Don was a good man."

"I'd like to say I knew him, but if I did, I don't remember."

The chief kept his eyes on me, but he didn't talk. Jack once told me the best way to make a suspect talk was to stare at them and not say a thing. It made them uncomfortable. I figured that was the chief's intent.

"He had trouble with some men at the park and came to you about it."

He crossed his arms over his chest and angled his head to the side. "Competitive coaches and fathers coming to check out the teams. Fairly common, but not illegal." He tapped his finger on his desk. "You're thinking this has something to do with the Bennett boy?"

"It's possible. The night Turner went missing, I saw Travis Bennett talking to a man toward the back of the lot. I didn't recognize him, and he looked like he'd been running. I can't say if he's from another team or not, but it's possible."

"People use that path for all sorts of things. Doesn't mean they're there to kidnap children."

"And it doesn't mean they aren't, either."

"Point taken."

I picked through my purse for my phone and clicked on the photos icon. "This is the door to the storage room under the bleachers. The coaches keep things in there. Balls, photos, previous seasons' playbooks, that kind of thing." I showed him the photo. "It looks like someone's tried to get the door open."

He examined the photo carefully. "Can you send that to me?"

I nodded. "Email?"

He gave me his email address, then said, "Could just be kids trying to get to the equipment."

"What if it has something to do with Turner's disappearance?"

He leaned back in his chair. "Anything's possible, I guess, but it's probably just kids."

"But what if it's not?"

"Taking equipment is one thing. Kidnapping a child is another. We're talking two different types of criminals."

"Or one who's escalated. It's at least worth further investigation."

He picked up his phone and spoke into it. "Get Hansen and Levitt to my office."

I toggled my phone between my hands as we waited. Chief Hagarty didn't say a word.

Officer Hansen and Jack walked in a minute later.

The chief nodded to Jack and then spoke to Officer Hansen. "You check the storage room under the bleachers?"

"We searched inside for the boy, sir."

Jack caught my eye.

The chief asked him about the items inside. "You got anything another team might consider valuable in there? Maybe old playbooks or something?"

"Personally, no, but that doesn't mean other coaches don't."

"Anything besides equipment stored in there?"

"Cleaning supplies, lawn maintenance products, that kind of thing."

I jumped in. "And rat poison."

Chief Hagarty furrowed his brow, then picked up his phone again. "Get me Buddy Jones at P&R, will ya?" He slammed the phone back into the receiver.

"There's also team photos on the wall," I said.

Jack nodded. "A few team shots of the last few seasons."

"The Bennett boy in those?"

"One," I said, before realizing he wasn't talking to me.

Officer Hansen stepped closer to the chief's desk. "Sir, we didn't find anything connected to the Bennett boy in the room."

The chief drew in a long breath. When he blew it out, his belly nudged the edge of the desk. "Hansen, anything can be connected to an investigation. Ms. Adair here showed me a photograph of the door frame. Looks like someone's tried to bust the lock. You see that when you looked for signs of the boy?"

Jack tried not to smile, but I could tell he wanted to.

"I don't believe we caught that, sir."

"I suggest you go back to the park and give that storage room a sweep."

"I told the chief there's rat poison on one of the shelves, but it's buried in the back."

Jack pursed his lips, and Officer Hansen narrowed her eyes at me. "You've been in the storage room?"

I nodded.

Her nostrils flared. "I'll send someone out while I finish talking to Detective Levitt, sir."

"I'll talk to Levitt. Take Pruitt with you. Go through everything. If you find any playbooks, or anything with the players' personal information, take it."

"But, sir, Levitt was the last—"

He cut her off. "Detective Levitt didn't take the kid, Hansen. Now go on, git."

She glared at Jack, but spoke to the chief. "Yes, sir."

CHAPTER 5

"They think my boy ran away." Charlotte sat at the corner table in Community Café. "He would never do that. I know my kid."

Del brought us each a cup of coffee. "On the house," she said, eyeing Charlotte.

She wouldn't charge me either, but I'd still pay. "Charlotte, this isn't Massachusetts. Small towns do things different, and we don't have those kinds of resources. Everyone is out looking for Turner. We'll find him, I promise."

"That officer keeps asking me about Coach Jack and his relationship with my son. I've told her he didn't do this. I know he didn't. He loves the kids, and I know Turner adored him."

She spoke of her son in the past tense. "Charlotte, when was the last time you slept?"

Tears streamed down her face. "I...I can't sleep."

I cupped my hand over hers. "Go home. Get some rest."

She held her head in her hands and cried. "My boy is gone. I don't know what to do."

I slipped into the chair beside her and patted her on the back. I could only imagine what she was going through, and I prayed it never happened to me. "You pray. That's all we can do right now."

She used the paper napkin to wipe her tears. Del quickly grabbed another one. Olivia arrived and sat with Thelma, who'd been sitting quietly—for a change—at the back corner table. Del poured her an iced tea and the three whispered together. Charlotte calmed down just as her husband walked in.

"Honey, we should get you home. Turner might show up, and you'll want to be there."

She stared at me with swollen, red eyes.

I nodded. "That's right. It's best you stay where he knows he can find you."

"That's what Officer Hansen said, but I've just felt so helpless."

"I know, but you're no good to your son in this state. Please, try to sleep."

Travis helped her up, wrapping his arm around her and letting her fall into him. "I don't know why that cop's so focused on your boyfriend," he said to me. "I keep telling her to talk to Bennett. He's involved." He walked her out before I asked what he meant.

I walked over to my friends.

Thelma sighed. "That poor woman."

Olivia watched them walk past the large picture window. "She's a hot mess for sure. What she's going through makes me not want kids."

"This kind of thing doesn't happen to most parents."

"Kids go missing every day," she said.

"You know what I mean." I sat in the chair between Olivia and Thelma, then leaned forward and whispered, "I might be interacting with someone who knows something and just can't tell me."

Three sets of eyes popped open. Del's included a jaw drop. "I'm out." She prefers dealing with the living over the dead. She's always been a trooper and stepped up when I've needed her, but usually only after a lot of pressure.

"Don't be such a party pooper," Thelma said.

"I'm no party pooper, I just don't want what happened last time to happen again. I need a few months to get over that one."

Thelma and Olivia glanced at each other. I gazed out the window, because I knew I'd start laughing when they looked at me. Del's last ghostly encounter didn't go well, and she hadn't let me forget it. We'd gone to visit an older Castleberry resident at the hospital, and while there, a very determined ghost pestered me the entire time. She wanted to get a message to a nurse, but I ignored her while we visited our friend. Ignoring a ghost isn't easy, especially the determined ones.

After several attempts to get my attention, she managed to fling a vase of roses from the table and sent them flying out of the room. I've never seen a woman Del's age run that fast in my whole life.

She bolted from the room and out of the hospital so fast an ambulance had to slam on its brakes and jerk to the left to avoid hitting her. Instead, it hit a police cruiser, and the person inside the ambulance flew from the stretcher. If not for the EMT's cushioned body, the patient would have landed on the floor. She was okay, but she broke the EMT's arm. The worst part was that while Del ran down the hospital hall, she thought she saw a ghost ahead of her and decided to run through it. It wasn't a ghost, it was a fragile old man with dementia who'd taken off his white gown and hadn't put it back on correctly.

"Ghosts don't wear hospital gowns," Thelma said.

I bit my lip.

Del jutted out her chin. "It looked like a sheet!"

"They don't wear sheets either," Olivia said.

I bent my head and chuckled.

"I can hear that," Del said.

"Sorry." I lifted my head and tried not to smile, but my face worked against me.

"Stop laughing. I'm not one of those mediums like you."

"No, you're definitely not."

If looks could kill, I'd be the one wearing the white sheet.

"That poor EMT, she had to wear that cast for six weeks," Olivia said, then chuckled too.

"Who's talking to you?" Thelma asked. "The boy? Is he dead?"

I shook my head. "Thank God. It's a maintenance man from the park. He died four years ago."

"You mean Mr. Rogers?" Olivia asked.

"You knew him?"

"Everyone in town knew Don. You've seen his ghost? You got to tell Mary. She'll be beside herself."

"There's nothing to tell, really. He's showed me things, but he's not talking." I shifted in my seat. "If he had a message for his wife, he probably would have said something by now."

"Sounds silly to me. You see the spirit, you should tell their loved ones," Del said.

Del's aware of Charlie's presence, and she knows he's not asking me to deliver any messages to Thelma. "If Mr. Rogers has something to say to his wife, he'll let me know."

"He hasn't said anything at all?" Thelma asked.

"Not a peep." I filled them in on what was going on.

"Oh, dear," Thelma said. "Why would that officer think Jack would hurt a kid?"

"She's just doing her job," I said, though I wondered if there was more to it.

"Maybe she's in love with him and he turned her down. I watched this movie on TV the other night about a woman whose husband left her for another woman. The wife pretended she was okay, even became friends with the new woman, and then she stabbed her in the back."

"Women do that all the time, they're nasty," Del said.

"No, I mean stabbed her with a knife. She killed her husband too."

Olivia winced. "Didn't I tell you to stop watching Lifetime?"

Thelma shrugged. "I didn't want to get up to change the channel."

"You have a remote," I said.

"Which I keep next to the TV."

Del, Olivia, and I collectively sighed. Sweet, sweet Thelma entertained us without intention.

"I don't think Officer Hansen has feelings for Jack," I said. "I think she's just doing her job, and since he was the last person to be seen with Turner, naturally he's going to be a person of interest."

"We know Jack. He wouldn't hurt a child," Del said.

"I know, and the chief knows that too."

"So, what do you think happened to the boy?" she asked.

Thelma raised her cup toward Del. "May I have another cup of coffee? This one's cold."

Del shook her head. "Can't you see we're talking here?"

"In a coffee shop, with cold coffee."

Del snatched the cup and charged to the kitchen. I waited for her to return before answering her question.

Thelma chuckled. "She throws a hissy fit as much as my cousin Henrietta switches man friends."

Olivia giggled. "Oh, wait! Henrietta? Does your cousin live in Bramblett?"

Thelma nodded. "How'd you know? I don't like to talk about her too much. She's a bit of a floozy."

I laughed. Way to throw your cousin under the bus, Thelma.

"She booked a haunted tour but had to cancel because of a bunion."

"Oh my. Bunions hurt." She shook her head. "If she tries to reschedule, tell her you're closed. She'll bring those people with her, and they'll ruin my reputation."

I coughed to cover my laugh.

Del returned with the coffee and set it in front of Thelma. "Where were we?"

"Thelma was telling us about her cousin ruining her reputation," Olivia said. Her tone was light and airy.

"That wasn't what we were talking about," I said.

Del held up a finger. "What reputation?"

"My good one. People in town respect me. I don't want my back-hills relatives tarnishing it."

Del shook her head. "Back-hills relatives? You wear Dolly Parton wigs and bright red lipstick, and you're worried about your reputation."

"That's part of my personal style."

"Anyway," I said, trying to get the conversation back on track. "I think Mr. Rogers is trying to show me that Turner's disappearance is somehow related to something that happened to him."

Del pulled a chair from the table next to us, flipped it around, and straddled it. "So, what's the plan?"

"Other than begging the ghost to speak, I don't have much of a plan."

"Have you talked to any of the parents?" Olivia asked.

"Not really. We have a text thread, but mostly it's prayers and empty updates."

Del's face lit up. "Why don't you call a meeting? Maybe someone's seen or heard something, and they don't know it. You can talk about what you've learned, and that might jar their memories."

"Tell them a ghost is showing me things?" I leaned back in my chair. "No thanks."

"You don't have to say how you've learned it, just that you know."

"She's right," Thelma said. "Del and I can serve coffee and water."

Olivia nodded. "You can bring them to the historical society. We have the space, and Thelma's right. They can serve coffee and snoop while people talk, because you know they're going to. And I can help too."

"Sounds like a good idea," Del said. "But I'm charging the city for the coffee."

I smirked. "I'll set it up."

Olivia offered to drive Thelma home, and I pulled Del aside. "What can you tell me about Mr. Rogers?"

"Other than he was a nice man?"

I nodded. "His wife said he had issues with some people coming to the fields and spying on the teams?"

"I don't know about that, but I do know he'd been feeling poorly the few days before his passing. Came in a few times but didn't get his regular order. He said he couldn't keep his food down, even coffee. Gave him some bitters and water, but he said it didn't help."

"Do you know what he died from?"

She glanced away and thought about it. "Can't say I do. Not even sure if anyone ever said."

"There had to have been an autopsy, right?"

She shrugged. "That you might could ask your ex-boyfriend. He should know."

∽

Jack stood in the corner of the historical society's large parlor. The Civil War-era beauty had seen many changes since I came on board, and was closer to its original style than ever. I loved the look. I adored the large windows and dark wood accents, and the curtains Thelma and I made were almost exact replicas of the ones from photos of the era.

During the Civil War, wealthy Southern women did what they could to maintain a certain status quo, which included wearing high-fashion dresses. When money got tight, they took drapes from destroyed homes, and sometimes their own, and made them into gowns. The drapes were thick and heavy, and I imagined the weight was tough on their bodies, but it gave them a sense of normalcy during the war. The problem was these dresses were attractive to soldiers, and the material was worth cash, so sometimes soldiers would raid the homes and take the clothing or drapes. This all happened before most of Atlanta burned, of course, but the stories I'd heard over the years, those passed down from family members as old wives' tales, said the women found ways to avenge the thefts.

No one messes with a woman and her clothing, no matter what era.

I walked over to Jack and hugged him. "I'm glad you're not in jail."

"At least someone is."

"What do you mean?"

"Hansen's not thrilled. If she had her way, she'd have me behind bars."

"She's an idiot."

A smile swept over his face. "I'm with you on that."

"Well." I adjusted my sleeve. "Let's get this started. Do you have anything to say?"

He shook his head. "I'm not allowed to talk about the investigation."

"Oh, all right then."

The group of parents gathered, everyone sipping coffee or tea from Del's place. She even brought her famous raspberry scones, which I knew she'd charge the city for too.

"Okay," I said, standing in front of the small crowd and clearing my throat. "In the past people from other teams have come to the park to scope out the competition. It's possible something like this is happening again. I'd like everyone to think about the park, the field, and what we've seen. I've asked everyone to list all their cars on this paper here." I held up the sheet. "So, if you haven't done so, please do. Also, if you've seen a car you didn't recognize, jot that down too. We'll give the list to the police and let them run with it."

Charlotte and Travis Hendricks walked in. Everyone turned and stared at them. I coughed to get the room's attention again. "Do any of you have any relationships with families from other teams?"

Bill Chatsworth leaned against the parlor's door frame with his arms crossed over his chest. "Are you trying to accuse one of us of something?"

That came out of left field. "Absolutely not. I'm trying to make a connection."

Officer Hansen walked in. When she saw Jack, she sneered and quickly looked at me. I acknowledged her with a slight head tilt.

"It sure sounds like you think we're doing something."

"Bill, I'm not accusing anyone of anything." I glanced at Officer Hansen. "What I'm doing is putting out information. I've come to learn competing teams could be scoping out our practices, and it's possible Turner Bennett was approached by one."

"You think he was abducted because of lacrosse?" one of the mothers asked.

"I don't know what to think. I'm just trying to gather information. If we put our heads together, we might think of something we didn't before or possibly make a new connection." The meeting took on a life of its own as the parents talked among themselves and compared mental notes.

Officer Hansen stood in the back watching.

Mr. Rogers walked through the closed door. The door opened, and a man with the ghost's eyes and stature walked in. His son.

"Everyone, please, can we focus here?"

No one paid attention to me. Jack kept back, his hands stuffed into his pockets, his left foot tapping the floor. I knew that stance, and I recognized his facial expression. Stiff jaw, still head, darting eyes. He was assessing the room and preparing his approach. With the crowd talking, and my inability to keep them focused, he'd jump in, whether he should or not.

Jack Levitt is a law enforcement officer to the core, and working with kids means the world to him. He once told me he wanted kids of his own but it wasn't in the cards. Volunteering gave him the chance to positively impact kids, and they loved him. I knew without question he wasn't involved in Turner's disappearance, and if Officer Hansen knew him at all, she'd understand that too.

The crowd mumbled and rumbled, their questions and theories filling the room. Jack stood by my side and held his hands in the air. He'd had enough. His voice was powerful, confident, and loud, and it commanded attention. "People, listen up. We won't get anything done like this. We all want to find Turner. Let's work together to make that happen."

The crowd simmered to a mumble here and there, their eyes glued to Jack.

Charlotte Hendricks leaned her weight against her husband. She'd tossed her graying hair into a clip, and it framed her face, highlighting the dark circles around her eyes. When he spoke, she wrapped her arms around his waist as if she couldn't stand on her own.

"Why would we tell you anything? You're a suspect."

Jack's shoulders stiffened. I placed my hand on his back.

"I'm not a suspect, Mr. Hendricks. What I am is a concerned coach, and I want to do whatever I can to find your son."

"You were the last person to see our son. Officer Hansen said you're a person of interest." He turned toward the female cop. "Why isn't he in jail?"

Several parents spoke at the same time.

"Coach would never hurt one of our kids."

"No way. Not Coach."

"He should be questioned like everyone else."

"Detective Levitt has been questioned and cleared," Officer Hansen said. She stepped toward Jack and me and faced the group. "We have no evidence to support Detective Levitt as a suspect in the disappearance of Turner Bennett. The department is actively pursuing other possibilities at this time. We appreciate all of you gathering to offer your support and work to find Turner Bennett, but accusations and anger won't bring him home any sooner."

John Bennett's voice boomed through the room. "What other possibilities? That means you don't have any suspects." He shifted toward his ex-wife and pointed at Travis Hendricks. "What about him?"

She shifted her stance, hooking her hands together behind her back. "I can't comment on an active investigation, sir."

His face reddened. "It's my son! I have a right to know what's going on."

Charlotte Hendricks stood on her own and her husband began to speak, but Officer Hansen cut him off. "Let's not do this here."

The rest of the room remained silent, their eyes glued to both men. I sucked in a breath and said a prayer they wouldn't fight. Expensive antiques from the Civil War lined the bookcases. If the two men fought, they could be destroyed.

Officer Hansen spoke calmly but with intent. "Mr. Bennett, perhaps this is a conversation we should have privately."

Jack's eyes met mine. We raised our eyebrows at the same time. I knew he wanted to jump in, but he wouldn't.

"I told you who's involved," John Bennett said. "Why haven't you arrested him?"

Mr. Rogers stood next to John Bennett. The ghost placed his hand on his shoulder, and John Bennett flinched. Had he felt it? The spirit's son had moved to a corner of the room. He leaned against the wall and watched the crowd with a smile spread across his face. I didn't see any humor in the situation.

Amanda Anderson, the mother of Avery, one of the team's middies, broke the few seconds of silence and eased the tension in the room. "I've seen men at the field. One's been there several times but he doesn't stay long." She made eye contact with a few of the parents. "He's really thin. I remember thinking he should eat more. Other than his weight, he didn't really stand out. He was dressed like all y'all. Beige shorts and a T-shirt."

I searched their faces for any signs of recognition and saw three. Hopefully Officer Hansen saw them too.

"Was he wearing a baseball cap?" I asked.

She shook her head. "Not when I've seen him. He's got short blond hair, though."

I glanced at Mr. Rogers and his son. Their tight jaws and half-closed eyes matched perfectly. They both knew the blond man.

Officer Hansen shifted her weight from one foot to the other, keeping her hands secured behind her and her shoulders back. "Let's talk when the meeting's over, and if anyone else recognizes that description, I'd appreciate you staying and talking with me too."

The meeting didn't exactly go as I'd planned, but we'd learned something, so I felt like it was successful. Officer Hansen and Jack stepped into the library and spoke privately while most of the group chatted for a few minutes and slowly filtered out.

Travis and John shot death stares at each other, but Charlotte convinced Travis to leave without a confrontation. My body relaxed now that I wouldn't have to explain the loss of expensive antiques to my board.

Del stuffed a stack of paper cups into a tote. I grabbed a bag of Stevia packets and set it inside the tote too.

"You ever see the skinny blond man?" she asked.

"I can't say for sure, but maybe." After making sure none of the parents could hear us, I whispered, "Mr. Rogers and his son were here. When Amanda mentioned him, they both tensed."

She dumped the basket of individual creamers into a plastic bag and tossed it into the tote. "He was here?"

"Yes, and he was visibly upset when Amanda mentioned the man. He knows who she's talking about."

She searched the room as she bagged the raw sugar packets. "But he's gone now?"

I rolled my eyes. "Yes, Del. He and his son both left."

She tried to hide her relief, but I caught it. Thelma shuffled toward the kitchen, carrying a small garbage bag over her shoulder. My eyes followed her. "When did she start shuffling like that?" I asked.

"I was going to ask you the same thing."

"That's not good."

Del nodded, but before we could talk more, Officer Hansen walked over. "Ms. Adair, I appreciate your desire to help, but if you decide to gather like this again, please let me know in advance."

I didn't bother asking how she found out, but I did tell her it wasn't my intent to exclude her. "We discovered a possible suspect, so I think it was beneficial."

"In my experience, these things often escalate quickly. I'm just glad I was here to keep it under control."

She was all of twenty-three. I didn't feel like she had a whole lot of experience in anything, let alone parental group gatherings about children.

I pacified her with a simple, "I understand."

Jack helped Olivia carry Del's totes to the car and came back inside after Officer Hansen left.

I wiped the table with a dry cloth. "What did she say?"

"She wanted my opinion, but went around the corner and over to Mississippi to ask."

I smirked. "Probably hurt her ego."

"She's young. She's got a lot to prove."

"At least she verified your innocence."

"True."

"Is it true there are no leads?"

"We have a potential suspect thanks to your efforts."

"I can't understand why no one mentioned him before." I sprayed a cleaner on the cloth and scrubbed a stain on the table. "And why we don't have security cameras at the park? I'm going to talk to the mayor about that."

"Spoken like a parent."

"Well come on, it's an obvious safety precaution."

"I'm sure the city will consider them now."

"I hope. What happens next?"

"The chief's got eyes on the field. They'll watch for the blond guy. If he acts suspicious, they'll talk to him."

"Won't they talk to him anyway?"

"Probably."

Jack spoke like he was part of the investigating team. "The biggest problem is the lack of evidence. We can't find any signs of violence or that Turner was taken against his will. All signs point to him either leaving on his own, or going with someone he knew."

"That's good, though. It narrows the suspect list."

He nodded. "And I know Hansen's looking into the parents."

"Family's always the first suspects."

"You're learning," he said, smiling. "If I were in charge, I'd meet with each parent again privately."

"About the blond guy?"

He nodded. "And Turner's parents."

I stopped what I was doing. "You think one of them did it."

"It's where I'd start."

"I'm sure the chief's had that discussion with Hansen."

"The chief is working closely with her."

"You should be handling this. You know what to do."

"Let's just say I'm involved without being involved." He winked.

"Good."

His cell phone beeped. When he read the message, he said, "I've got to go. Can we talk later?"

I hugged him. "Definitely."

As he walked out, Olivia walked back in. "Chantilly, there's someone to see you." Mr. Rogers's son walked in behind her.

I thought he'd left, but I was wrong.

"You're his son," I said, smiling.

"I'm sorry?" Don Junior was about my age, with thinning hair, and in fairly good shape. I imagined his father looked similar at our age.

I ignored the implied question. "You were here for the meeting."

The ghost walked over and stood next to his son. "My name is Don Rogers. My father was a maintenance man at the park."

"Yes, I know of your dad. I'm sorry for your loss." The loss of a loved one never disappeared, and since I knew how it felt, I always offered my condolences, and I meant them.

He nodded. "Thank you. I just talked to the officer outside, but she wasn't too interested in what I had to say."

"Would you like something to drink?"

He shook his head. "I'm fine, thanks."

"Let's have a seat." We'd moved all the furniture against the parlor walls and hadn't put them back, but the small library was a lovely place to sit, so we walked over there. "What did you tell her?"

I had no idea why he'd chosen to talk to me, but I was glad he did.

He sat in the blue and white striped chair across from me. "My father had some issues with competitive teams and the parents coming to the park."

"I wasn't back in town when that happened, but I've heard about it."

"Yeah, well, pretty soon he realized the same men were at games too, and their teams were winning. Our teams were all mostly undefeated at the time. He realized the men were stealing the plays and figuring out how to play against them. When they started talking to the kids, he said something to our teams' coaches. I guess one coach said he'd talk to one of the other team coaches, but that just made it worse."

"How do you mean?"

"We think our coach told the other one my father had said something, because they started harassing him, and they stepped up their game with the players. Dad said they talked to them before and after practices and even talked to the parents." He took a breath.

"My dad tried talking to one of the men. I don't know for sure, but I think it was the one the woman here mentioned."

"Did that help?"

"Just made it worse. Little things started happening to my dad. His truck was keyed. The storage room where parks and rec kept maintenance supplies was broken into. Dad finally put a padlock on the door. They couldn't break that."

"That's awful."

"It didn't stop there. They found out where my parents live and would do stupid stuff like ding-dong ditch and egg the house."

"Are you sure it was them?"

He nodded. "They left notes on the car. 'Back off, we're watching you,' that kind of thing."

"Did your mother know about this?" If so, she didn't tell me.

"He blamed kids in the neighborhood."

"So she didn't know about the notes?"

"He didn't want her to worry."

"But he told you."

"He was scared."

"I know he told the Castleberry police about the harassment. Did he contact the Dahlonega police about the house?"

"Hagarty said he'd take care of it."

The spirit stepped behind his son. "You don't think he did, do you?" I was talking to the spirit, but his son obviously didn't know that.

Don Junior shook his head. "Even if he did, it was too late. Dad was already sick. Two days after he told me about the notes, he was gone."

"That's terrible. I'm so sorry. With all that going on, why no autopsy?"

His stiff jaw, tense shoulders, and locked knees showed his anger. "My mother didn't want it. It took some convincing, but Hagarty got the coroner to release him without one. Mom just wanted my dad to rest in peace."

Roaming the lacrosse park didn't seem like resting in peace to me.

He sighed. "I think the men who harassed my dad—no, the men who murdered my dad—took that kid."

Lacrosse practice continued without Turner. A few parents worried about their kids' safety and wanted to cancel, but with the big tournament approaching, the kids begged to practice. They thought Turner would want them to play, and they wanted to *kick some serious lacrosse butt* in his honor. How could we refuse?

Every parent went to practice and watched the area like hawks waiting to attack. Nothing stopped a child abductor like a group of hypersensitive parents.

I hung out near the storage room and researched the competing teams on the internet while keeping my eye out for

Mr. Rogers. I found news articles from our local paper honoring the scholarship recipients from our teams but nothing similar for the competitors.

Bill Chatsworth yelled at his son on the field. "Go for the goal, William! Go for the goal!"

I scooted to the edge of the bleachers and watched the team scrimmage. William played Turner's position, and defense wasn't supposed to shoot on goal unless their shot was clear and open. Midfielder defensemen, or middies for short, were supposed to keep the other team from scoring and get the ball to their attacks. A middie who ran the field and shot did so for glory, not for the team.

Bill Chatsworth put so much pressure on his son he'd made him into a ball hog. Lacrosse parents, especially the fathers, could be tough on their kids. Every parent thought their kid would get a lacrosse scholarship to a big college like Duke, but the chances of that, especially in Castleberry, Georgia, were slim to none.

I appreciated my son's approach. He loved the game and had no desire to play in college. He was good, but not enough for a scholarship, and that was fine with us.

I rolled my eyes as Bill Chatsworth jogged the length of the fence, following his son down the field. Most of the parents ignored him, but a few looked like they wanted to punch him in the face.

A cold brush of air circled around me. I exhaled, seeing my breath, and then rushed back to the storage room. I made sure no one was behind me and smiled at Mr. Rogers, who was standing near the door. I removed the key from the box and unlocked the padlock. "The padlock trick's pretty cool," I whispered. "I'd love to know how you pulled it off."

He smiled.

I closed the door behind us and flipped on the light. "The skinny blond man, he has Turner, doesn't he?"

He closed his eyes and dropped his chin toward his chest. When he looked back at me, the sadness on his face tore at my heartstrings.

He still wasn't up for talking. "Is Turner okay?"

His face stayed neutral. "Okay, you don't look upset, so I'll take that as a yes." I leaned against the wall. "How about this, do you know where he is?" I waved my hands. "I can ask yes or no questions if you'll nod or shake your head."

Of course he did neither.

I groaned and ran my hand through my hair. "I don't know what to do," I pleaded. "Please. I know I can help you if you'll just talk to me."

He pointed at me.

"Me? I...I don't understand."

He pointed at me again and then at himself.

My chest tightened. "What are you—I don't know what you're trying to tell me."

He just kept pointing.

I rubbed my neck. "Okay, let me think." I paced up and down the small space. "What do we have in common? Lacrosse." I nodded as I rotated on my heels and paced toward the door again. "The park. Lacrosse." We made eye contact. "What could a living middle-aged woman have in common with a dead man?"

His eyes widened.

I jabbed my finger at him. "That's it? Are you trying to tell me Turner's dead like you?"

He pointed at me again.

My heart raced. "He's alive? That's it, isn't it?"

He finally dropped his hand.

I closed my eyes and exhaled. "Dear God in heaven, thank you." When I opened them, the ghost was gone.

A plastic bottle fell off the shelf. I picked it up to put it back, and stared at the container of rat poison. That tub was somehow connected to everything, and I was determined to find out how.

As I stepped out of the storage room, a man I didn't recognize rushed by. I zipped around to the parking lot and watched him get into a black SUV. I dug in my purse for my phone, chiding myself for having everything but the kitchen sink in there. By the time I found it in the interior side pocket, the SUV was gone. The driver was thin and wore a baseball cap, but I couldn't tell if he was the same man I saw talking to Travis Hendricks.

I climbed the bleachers and sat next to Amanda. "A man just ran by me. He was skinny and wore a baseball cap. I tried to get a picture of him, but I couldn't. He got in a black SUV. Did you see him?"

She shook her head and pointed at Bill Chatsworth. "Numb wad down there keeps distracting me. Did you call Officer Hansen?"

I bit my lip. "I wanted to check with you first, but I will."

"I did keep an eye out before, but I haven't seen anyone. I'll try to stop focusing on Chatsworth's big mouth and keep an eye out again."

"I think I'll try to get Bill to chill out."

She nodded. "Good luck with that."

I walked to the storage room side of the field and leaned against the fence. Chatsworth headed my direction, hollering at the team. I eyed Jack and caught him glaring at Bill.

Chatsworth stopped walking when Jack blew the whistle and the team froze. Before I could get to him, John Bennett tapped me on the shoulder. The shock kicked my heartrate up several notches. "John, did you find Turner?"

He shook his head. "Nothing."

I touched his arm. "Don't give up hope."

He watched Jack talk to the boys. "William's starting now. Chatsworth's probably drooling about that." His nostrils flared.

"Don't go there."

He flicked his head toward Bill. "He's said stuff to my kid. Told him he couldn't cradle the ball. Said his son had a better shot." His head shifted toward Bill and then back to the field, his jaw tightening.

"He just wants his son to play more."

"Bad enough to hurt my kid?"

"I don't know if—"

He cut me off. "I told the cops what he said to my kid. They said they talked to him, but he's got an alibi."

"Bill's a jerk, but I don't think he'd hurt a child."

He faced me, his eyes narrowed into thin slits. "Desperate people do desperate things."

He went to turn toward Bill again, but I grabbed his arm and squeezed. "Let the police handle this."

He exhaled. "They aren't doing anything."

I tightened my grip. "Go home. I'll talk to Bill. If he says anything suspicious, I'll call Officer Hansen. It'll be better coming from me. Please, just go home. You don't need to get in trouble."

It took more begging on my part, but I finally convinced him to leave.

I casually walked toward Bill Chatsworth and tapped him on the shoulder. "William's playing well today."

He nodded. "Should have been the starting middie from day one."

"I'm pretty sure everyone knows you feel that way."

He shifted his head from the field to me. "What's that supposed to mean?"

"I know you're glad William's the starting middie, and yes, he's a good player, one of the best on the team. But given the circumstances, maybe you should dial down the enthusiasm a bit?"

"I got a right to be proud of my kid."

"Of course you do. But things are pretty intense right now, and I think it's making some of the parents uncomfortable, and

I'm worried it might make William look bad to the other players."

"I'll tell you what. You take care of your kid, and I'll take care of mine."

The man tested my patience. "Your son isn't starting in the tournament because he earned that spot. He's starting because Turner Bennett is missing." His eyes shot daggers into me, but I didn't falter. "Has it occurred to you how this looks, you acting like this?"

He took a step back. "You accusing me of doing harm to that boy?"

"I'm saying your behavior is suspect." I wiggled my toes in my shoes to calm my nervous energy.

Bill's face reddened, and spittle flew from his mouth as he spoke. "You watch yourself, Ms. Adair."

"I am watching myself." I pointed at the parents in the bleachers. "And so are they." I stepped back and flipped around. As I walked away, I made eye contact with several dads in the stands.

I sat at the far end of the bleachers and kept my head down, checking my phone. When it came to that fight-or-flight concept, I always chose fight, but I wasn't stupid. Egging on Bill Chatsworth was dangerous enough, but giving him the opportunity to take it to the next level wasn't an option.

Tim Jacobs, one of the team dads, sat next to me. "You okay?"

"I'm fine. He's a jerk."

"Yeah, he is, but we got your back. We'll make sure he's gone right quick at the end of practice."

"I appreciate that."

Bill Chatsworth just put himself on my mental suspect list.

CHAPTER 6

Tim kept his word. He and two other dads got Bill to leave without incident. I hung back while Austin helped Jack clean up.

Austin loved Jack, and I wished things had turned out differently between us. Scott lived in Birmingham, and although Austin saw him once a month, he was still young and needed a strong male presence in his life. Jack had been that. I prayed ending our relationship wouldn't take its toll on theirs.

Austin dropped his bag next to me. "I'm starving. Can I go to McDonald's with the Merritts?"

I sighed. I'd taken the time to prepare a white chicken chili and it was warming in the Crock-Pot at home. "I made dinner."

"Please, Mom."

"Come straight home after, okay?"

"Yes, ma'am." He yanked his bag from the ground, hollered, "I can go," and jogged to Kyle Merritt.

I sent Kyle's mom a text. "Keep an eye on my boy, please."

She sent back a thumbs-up emoji.

Jack bumped my shoulder with his. "Chatsworth giving you a hard time?"

"He's just being his usual jerk self."

"I'll have a talk with him." He walked to the storage room and unlocked the door with his key.

I leaned against the door frame. "Do you think he could have hurt Turner?"

"Are you asking Coach Jack or Detective Levitt?"

I smiled. "Whichever one gives me the most informed answer."

"It's possible. Chatsworth likes to yell and throw his weight around, but I don't think he'd hurt another kid."

"That's what I thought at first, but John Bennett said something that made me think."

He put the bag of balls in a storage bin. "What's that?"

"'Desperate people do desperate things' or something to that effect."

"He's right."

"And it got me thinking. Remember that woman in Texas? The one who killed a girl on a cheerleading team because she made the team and her daughter didn't? If a mother could do it, Chatsworth could too."

"The mother didn't kill anyone. She tried to hire a hitman to kill the mother of the child who got the spot on the team. Thankfully, the hitman ended up being an undercover cop."

"Why aren't you handling the investigation now? You've been cleared. I don't see any reason why you can't."

He wiped the sweat on his forehead with a towel. "If I get involved and someone is arrested, a defense attorney would tear the case apart. It doesn't matter if I'm cleared or not, I have to stay on the sidelines for this. Hansen's green, but like I said before, the chief's on it. They'll find Turner, or they'll figure out who took him."

"I don't like the way you phrased that."

"Neither do I, but we have to face the facts. It's been a few days. No calls for ransom. A few sightings, but nothing credible. Either he's run away, which I highly doubt, or he went with someone he knew. And if that's the case, it doesn't look good."

His hip brushed against mine as he walked past. He held the door open with his back. "After you, ma'am."

He locked the door and pulled on it to make sure it was secure.

"A man was here earlier, but I couldn't get a good look at him. He was skinny and wore a baseball cap. I think it's the guy Amanda mentioned."

He furrowed his brow. "Did anyone else see him?"

"I only asked Amanda. Chatsworth was distracting, and then John Bennett showed up and I wanted to keep him calm, and honestly, I just forgot." He cringed. "He left in a black SUV, though. I can call Hansen and let her know."

"I've got it."

He walked me to my car and stepped toward me as I opened the door. Before, he would have kissed me, and a very big part of me hoped that he would, but he didn't. It was disappointing, but if I didn't realize I wanted that, how could he?

Jack and I shared something honest and real, and that kind of love didn't just stop because the relationship ended. I'd been mad, but I wasn't anymore. Turner's disappearance took so much emotional energy, I didn't have any left to channel anger toward Jack. It was a step in the right direction.

~

"You do not." Del's voice shook as she spoke over the line. "I can't think of anything else to do. Something's holding him back. He knows something, and if I could just get him to talk, I might be able to find Turner."

"What makes you think hanging out at his grave will get him talking?"

"Nothing. Everything. I don't know, but it's worth a shot. Maybe being close to his body will give him strength."

"Being around a ghost is bad enough, but a cemetery? I don't need to see any ghosts from the graves. That'll give me a heart attack for sure."

"Your heart is fine."

"You don't know that."

"You showed me your EKG, remember?"

"That's not the point. I don't like those séances. You know that."

"You're the one who suggested the first one."

"And I regret that."

"Del, please. I'm better at all this now. I promise it'll be fine. You're the strongest woman I know."

"Bless your heart, you need to make more friends."

I laughed. "Is that a yes?"

"What's it called when the police talk to someone who doesn't want to talk?"

"Duress?"

"That's it. Fine, I'll do it, but under duress."

I shook my fist. "Thank you! I'll pick you up in twenty minutes."

"Wait a minute. You want to do it tonight?"

"Desperate people do desperate things."

I knew Del would agree to go, duress or no duress, so I'd already put all of my séance supplies in the back of my car. It wasn't much, just a blanket, some candles and matches, and sage wrapped in tissue. The sage resembled an extra-fat, extra-long cigar.

I didn't tell her, but I despised séances as much as Del did. I'd only done one before tonight, and I prayed this one would be the last.

Austin sat on the couch in the den playing video games. I watched a cartoon man dressed in military clothes shoot at the window of a building. I hate video games, but Scott loved them, and he'd created a monster in our son. I'd planned to not allow them in the house after we moved, but I gave in without Austin knowing my plan. His life had changed enough, and I didn't have the heart to change it more.

I plucked the earphones from his right ear and told him I had to help Del with something and not to wait up.

Olivia agreed to grab Thelma and meet Del and me at the cemetery.

Del got in the car and rambled on and on for the five-minute drive. "My palms are sweating." She swiped her hand down her neck. "My neck's sweating. By the time this is over, I'll need another shower."

"I appreciate you doing this."

When we reached the cemetery, she stepped out of my car but wouldn't let go of the door handle. "I've changed my mind. Take me home."

"Close the door, please. You don't want any ghosts hitching a ride back to your place, do you?"

She slammed the door shut while I chuckled under my breath.

Olivia parked next to me. I opened the passenger door to help Thelma out and had to look away. Bless her heart. Thelma was a trooper. "So, that's your secret to glowing skin!"

Del coughed. "She's going to scare the ghosts away."

Olivia clicked the lock on her key fob. "I think Miss Thelma is beautiful on the inside and out."

Thelma touched the dried green mask on her face. It cracked as she spoke. "It's supposed to stay on for twenty minutes. I didn't have time to take it off."

"She showed me the box. I told her we could take it off, but she didn't want to make y'all wait."

Del chuckled. "That and the shower cap on top of her head will look mighty pretty in her mugshot."

I rolled my eyes. "Must you?"

She laughed. "Can't help myself. The words just come out without me even thinking them."

That garnered her another eye roll as I popped open the back of my car. I handed Olivia a large quilt. "Can you carry this and I'll get the box of candles?"

"Sure thing," she said.

I locked my car and followed the path toward Mr. Rogers's grave. "Follow me, ladies."

"I don't get it. Why're we doing this here if you've seen him at the park? Aren't you afraid of waking more of the dead?"

Maybe, but I certainly didn't want to tell Del that. "There's a lot of different theories on this, but I feel like if we do the séance here, he won't be distracted by the park. Something's keeping him focused on that, yes, but he's so focused, I can't get anything from him. Maybe it'll be different here."

Olivia adjusted the quilt in her arms. "What if he doesn't show?"

"Just pray he does."

Del lagged a few feet behind me and Olivia. "I can think of a hundred other things I'd rather be doing right now."

Thelma suggested Del go home with her for a facial after the séance. "We can have a spa night."

I swallowed hard so I wouldn't laugh.

"I'd rather have my teeth pulled without that numbing stuff than give myself a facial."

"But they're so good for your skin," Olivia said.

"My momma used to skin the fish daddy would catch and rub the insides on my face. Said it helped with pimples. I'm still getting over that."

That got a laugh out of all of us.

"My momma just used cod liver oil," Thelma said.

"It's the same thing," Olivia said.

Del grunted.

I stood in front of Mr. Rogers's grave. "We're here."

We all took a moment as Del prayed. "Dear Lord, please let this man rest in peace. But before you do, Chantilly here's going to need some information from him. It's for the missing boy. Amen."

"Amen," I said.

Olivia spread out the quilt and helped Thelma sit down.

"I should have brought one of my lawn chairs. I'm going to have a heck of a time getting up."

Olivia sat Indian-style next to her. "Don't worry, Miss Thelma. We've got you covered." She glanced up at Del. "Need some help?"

Del groaned as she slowly sat on the quilt. "I'm not as old as that one. I can do it myself."

I lit the candles and placed them in a small circle in the center of the quilt. We set up on the blacktop path in front of Mr. Rogers's tombstone instead of the grass. It just felt wrong to sit on someone's burial site.

I took Del's and Thelma's hands. "No peeking this time." I popped my left eye open and caught Thelma wide-eyed. "Thelma?"

"Oh goodness, you caught me red-handed. Sorry."

"Okay, I need y'all to focus on Mr. Rogers."

"I remember him," Olivia said. "He was such a nice old man."

"He wasn't old," Thelma said.

"Oh hush now," Del said. "Compared to Olivia, we're all old."

"Maybe you, but I'm young at heart."

I leaned my head back and sighed. "Ladies?"

"Fine," Del said. "We got to hurry up anyway."

"Yes, I have to go potty," Thelma said. "And my face is really itchy."

"Okay. Here we go." I cleared my throat and pictured the man's spirit as I saw him at the park. "Donald Rogers, I need your help. Please, if you're here, show yourself."

Del tightened her hold on my hand. An owl hooted and she squeezed harder.

I pushed back on her tight grip. "That hurts."

She relaxed.

I did a quick eye check, and Thelma smiled at me. "Thelma! Close your eyes!"

"Oh! They just opened on their own." She shut them again.

I took another deep breath and started over. "Donald Rogers, please show yourself."

Chills crawled up my spine, and the hairs on the back of my neck stood. The temperature dropped quickly. Del squeezed my hand hard again.

"Oh boy," Thelma said.

I opened my eyes, expecting to see Mr. Rogers standing close by, but he wasn't there. A woman wearing a floor-length red dress took a step toward us. The dress's poufy sleeves and shoulders, the simple round collar, and the crinoline petticoat were fashion trends during the Civil War era. I kept my voice low. "Hello."

Thelma's voice shook with excitement. "Is he here? Don, is that you?"

"It's not him," I whispered.

"Well heck," Del said. "It's a demon. We're all gonna die."

Thelma's eyes popped open. "Oh, thank God. I thought it might be a zombie."

Del kept her eyes closed and shook her head. "You aren't worried about a demon, but you're worried about a zombie?"

"I saw them on TV and read that show is filmed in Atlanta. They could come up this way."

"Bless her heart. She's gone crazy right here in this cemetery," Del said.

Olivia kept quiet.

"Ladies, hush."

The woman was beautiful. Her long dark hair, pulled back

into a braid that hung past her waist, highlighted her pale complexion and deep blue eyes. She was young, probably no more than twenty when she passed. Disease was common during her life, and simple things like diarrhea killed people.

The woman stared at me.

"My name is Chantilly."

She stood outside our circle near an old faded tombstone. I couldn't make out what it said. "Is that yours?"

Her lips trembled and she shook uncontrollably.

"It's okay. I can help you."

Her eyes widened as her jaw fell open. A high-pitched scream sent sharp pains through my ear canals. I squeezed my eyes shut, bent my head, and covered my ears, praying she would stop. "Stop it!" I yelled. "You're hurting me!"

The pain only lasted a few seconds, but it felt like hours. When I opened my eyes, she was gone. I breathed deeply. "Heaven help that young woman."

"What happened?" Olivia asked.

Del rocked back and tried to stand. The rocking gave her momentum, but she lost her balance and her bum hit the ground hard. "Someone help me up. Let's get out of here. Lord knows what'll follow us home."

Another burst of ice-cold air swept over us.

"Not again," she said, taking my hand and holding on for dear life.

"Close your eyes, quick!" I said as I squeezed mine shut. Once the air warmed up, I opened them. "It's him."

"Heaven help us," Del said.

Thelma added, "And keep us safe from the flesh-eating zombies."

Mr. Rogers wasn't smiling. Instead he furrowed his brow and tilted his head.

"I thought maybe you'd be able to talk near your...your body." I shrugged. "Desperate people do desperate things."

The ground began to spin. I let go of Thelma's and Del's hands and pressed my palms into the ground to steady myself. I couldn't prepare myself for what was about to happen, and I didn't care. I just needed answers. I was dizzy and lightheaded. A light sheen of sweat glistened over my skin. I closed my eyes and relaxed, letting the spin take me where he wanted me to go. I opened my eyes as the spinning slowed. I wasn't at the cemetery anymore. He'd taken me back to the storage room. But I wasn't alone.

The room was a fuzzy blur, but I saw the two men well enough to recognize one from his body shape. I focused on their faces, but no matter how hard I tried, they were too blurred to make out. I scanned the room but didn't see Mr. Rogers anywhere.

I watched as one man lifted a small red cooler from the ground and placed it on a blue storage tub. He wasn't that tall, maybe five foot eight tops, and he was shaped like a potato. He opened the cooler and removed a thermos, then unscrewed the lid and set it on the storage tub.

The skinny man slipped on a pair of medical-style latex gloves and then moved a bottle on the middle shelf. He carefully removed the container of rat poison, opened it, and removed several small pellets from inside. He dropped the pellets into the cooler and placed everything back where he'd found it while the other man returned the thermos to the cooler. They were in and out in just a few minutes.

It all played out like a movie. I was there, but I wasn't part of the events. I followed the men outside and watched as they got into a black SUV. Just then, Mr. Rogers walked around the bleachers.

I rushed over to him, begging him not to go into the storage room, but my begging fell on deaf ears. He opened the cooler and then the thermos. As he brought the thermos to his mouth, I pleaded with him to hear me, to stop before it was too late. "Mr. Rogers, no! Don't drink it! It's poison!"

It was useless. I watched him swallow God only knew how much poison, and I fell to my knees and cried. "Oh my God, they killed you." Tears dripped from my eyes while I watched in horror as he finished the rest of the drink. I dragged my hands down my face and rocked in place. "Oh my God. Oh my God. Oh my God."

"It's okay, honey." Olivia was sitting next to me and holding me close. "It's all going to be okay."

I stopped rocking, but I couldn't stop crying. "They killed him."

Olivia tightened her hold on me and let me cry.

Del had a coffee and raspberry scone waiting for me when I arrived. "How you holding up?"

I closed my eyes and pressed my lips together, praying I wouldn't burst into tears again. "I don't want to do this anymore. I can't do this anymore."

She pulled me into a hug. "Yes, you can. You're stronger than the strongest person you know."

I cried into her shoulder.

The Community Café door opened, and I pushed away from Del, wiping my face and hoping to go unnoticed.

Del coughed, then flicked her head slightly toward the door. "Get it together," she whispered.

I took a deep breath and ducked my head as I grabbed the coffee and scone, then turned around and bumped right into Jack.

"Hey, you okay?"

I sucked in a breath, worried if I tried to talk I'd end up in tears again.

Del jumped in and covered for me. "She's having a tough day. The missing boy's wearing on her."

"It's wearing on all of us," he said. He blocked me from leaving, and tipped my chin up with his finger. "Everything's going to be okay." He kissed my forehead.

I choked back the tears. He was wrong. Everything wouldn't be okay. Mr. Rogers was murdered, and I knew the men who did it were the same men who took Turner. I couldn't shake the feeling he was dead too, and I stayed up all night trying to get his spirit to come to me.

It never did.

But I couldn't tell Jack any of that because he didn't know about my gift. Jack spends his days looking at facts, and there are no facts to support a person seeing spirits. I'd wanted him to know the truth, but I wouldn't risk our relationship over it.

"I know," I lied.

"We got a credible hit on the tip line, but we hit a dead end."

"A credible tip?"

"Someone saw a kid matching Turner's description in Alpharetta."

I took two steps back to put some distance between us. "But it wasn't him?"

"We don't know. Alpharetta PD searched the area but couldn't find the kid."

"You're talking like you're involved with the investigation now. Has something changed?"

He shook his head. "Chief keeps me updated."

"Oh."

Del brought him a drink. "Black with two sugars." He tried to pay her but she wouldn't take it. "Your money's no good here."

He tossed a ten-dollar bill on the table near us. "Consider that a tip then."

She swiped the bill into her hand and tucked it inside her bra.

Jack raised an eyebrow. I just shrugged then sighed.

"You're not going to work, are you?"

"I have to. I've barely been there. I've got requests piling up on my desk."

"May I walk you?"

"Sure."

We took our time walking the short block to the historical society. The awkwardness that had settled between us after he unceremoniously dumped me was almost gone, and things felt close to normal. I couldn't look into his hazel eyes, see the five o'clock shadow framing his jaw, or brush against his broad shoulders without feeling butterflies in my stomach.

He stepped through the historical society doors. "You sure you're okay?"

"I just need to focus on something else for a while."

He kissed my forehead again. "I'll call you when there's an update."

I climbed the stairs slowly as visions of Mr. Rogers's death flashed through my mind. Olivia hollered hello from down the hall and met me in my office.

Her smile faded when she saw my face. "Did you sleep at all?"

I shook my head.

"I'm so sorry. Have you seen him today?"

"No, but I haven't been to the park either. I just can't. Not yet."

"Oh honey, I understand. I feel awful for you. What can I do to help?"

"I'm going to go through this stack of requests. I'd like to try to get some sleep after I finish. Do we have any tours scheduled today?"

"No, ma'am, and Thelma's insisted I'm to call her right quick if her cousin calls again." She shivered. "Bunions. Gross."

I made it through all ten requests without falling asleep. Three cups of coffee gave me false energy, and so I decided to use it to my advantage. Mr. Rogers picked me to tell the truth, and I refused to let him down.

The woman behind the glass partition nodded. "I'll see if he's available."

Chief Hagarty walked into the reception area. His smile turned into a frown when our eyes met. "Is everything okay?"

"Not really. Can we talk?"

"Sure, come on back." He pointed at the woman behind the glass. "Hold my calls, please."

"Yes, Chief."

"Please don't let me down," I whispered to the young ghost walking next to me.

The chief moved a seat out from the table near his desk. "Please, have a seat." He sat next to me. "This has been hard on all of us, and I know you've tried to help. I wish I had some answers for you, but I don't."

My stomach did a somersault. I took a breath and prayed my plan would work. "I have something to tell you."

CHAPTER 7

"I...I'm..." He shook his head, his mouth hanging open. "I know it sounds crazy, but I can prove it."

He picked up a pencil and tapped the eraser on the table. "You can prove it?"

Chief Hagarty's son laughed. "This ought to be good." He walked to his father's desk and leaned against the corner. "Tell him ghosts are nothing compared to the monsters walking around the real world."

I twisted my fingers together and dug my nails into my palms. "Ghosts are nothing compared to the monsters walking around."

He blinked. "Where—how—" His shoulders stiffened. "Is this some kind of game?"

I shook my head slowly. "No, sir."

Steve Junior stepped behind his father. "Tell him I lied about the car. I hit a light post in the school parking lot."

I quickly repeated what he said.

The chief leaned forward and studied me carefully. "You're serious."

"Yes." I tapped my foot on the carpet.

He scanned the room, paying extra attention to the ceiling. "Is this some kind of retirement joke? Who put you up to this?"

Steve Junior shrugged. "If I focus hard enough, I think I can move his pencil."

I shook my head slightly. "No one put me up to this, Chief. It's not a joke."

"It's not a joke?"

"No, sir."

"No one's filming this?"

"Not that I'm aware of."

His body relaxed, and his eyes softened. "Then I think you should head on over to the doctor right quick. I've read about this kind of thing. Brain tumors can cause hallucinations."

"I don't have a brain tumor." I rubbed my temples. "Chief, I've been to the hospital. I've had several X-rays, two CT scans, and two independent MRIs. There's nothing wrong with my brain. This all started when I fell down the stairs at work. A few days later I saw Agnes Hamilton swinging from the rafters at the Hamilton House. I wasn't hallucinating then, and I'm not now. Your son is here, but he's not the reason I'm telling you this."

The spirit tossed his arms in the air. "Dude, way to suck the life out of my return."

I glared at him.

"Chill out, I'm just messing with you." He placed his hands on his father's shoulders.

Chief Hagarty jumped from his seat and backed up against his desk. "I...I..."

"You felt that, didn't you? That was your son's hands on your shoulders."

He shook his head. "I should have retired last year. I could be living on the lake in Michigan now."

Steve Junior leaned against the desk next to his father. "Tell him to make sure he digs up the time capsule, and tell him I'll be there when he does."

"Is it in Michigan?" I asked.

He nodded.

"What're—"

I interrupted the chief. "He wants to make sure you get the time capsule. He said he'll be there with you when you dig it up."

His eyes widened and he made the sign of the cross over his chest.

Steve Junior laughed. "We're not Catholic."

The chief dragged his hand down the side of his face.

His son moved in front of him. "We had a fight. It was stupid. I was stupid. Mom cried, and I don't know, I just couldn't deal, you know, so I took off. I didn't get far. I hitched a ride and that was it. Later, after I, you know…I went home. I didn't know what to do."

I swallowed the lump in my throat.

"They were arguing. Mom told him she wanted a divorce. Said she was going to see the judge in the morning. When I didn't come home that night, or the next day, I guess the divorce didn't matter anymore."

I cried as I told his son's story. The chief cried too.

"We never talked about divorcing again."

"He's glad for that."

"And tell him I came clean about the fish."

Steve Junior laughed. "I knew he'd tell Mom." He told me the story. "The fish." He nodded. "The first time we went fishing, I was about five or six, I think. I told my mom I'd bring her home something to cook for dinner, only I didn't catch a thing. Dad didn't either. I was bummed. We walked to the car and there was this guy putting a hook full of fish into a cooler attached to the back of his truck. My dad told me to wait in the car. A few minutes later he came back with two largemouth bass. He told me we'd let Mom think we caught them and it would be our secret." He smiled at the memory. "I bet he dropped at least twenty on those fish."

I smiled. "He thinks you paid twenty dollars for the fish."

Chief Hagarty turned around and walked the few steps back to his seat. He dropped into it and caught his breath. "Fifty bucks. Those things cost me fifty bucks."

Steve Junior laughed hysterically. "Golden!"

A tear fell from the chief's eye. He wiped his face and coughed, then his expression turned serious. "Does he know who—"

"Tell him I'm okay."

"He won't say."

"But we can get justice—"

"The guy can't hurt anyone anymore."

"Chantilly, I don't know what to say. I'm—"

"Chief, there's more, but first, I need you to promise not to say anything to Jack about this, okay?"

"Does he know you can—"

I shook my head. "And I should be the one to tell him."

He nodded. "Yes, right. Of course."

"Thank you."

"I'm the one who should be thanking you. I'm—"

"Like I said, there's more. I know what happened to Donald Rogers, and I think it's connected to Turner's disappearance."

n older woman with gorgeous, light-toned skin led me to Don Junior's office. "Mr. Rogers will be with you shortly. Can I get you something to drink?"

"I'm fine, thank you."

She closed the door behind her as she left. I admired the bear sculpture on the side of his desk. The painting over the corner table looked familiar. I typed its description into the browser on my phone and nodded. My job required I know a little about a lot, and it felt good to see I was right.

"Ms. Adair, sorry to keep you waiting." He pulled out the chair against the wall and sat.

I pointed behind him. "Is that a Pirosmani?"

"The photo? No idea. I bought it at an estate sale in Buckhead."

"May I ask how much you paid?"

"I don't remember, but I'm pretty cheap, so probably less than a few hundred bucks."

"You should have it checked. If it's an original it could be worth a lot more than that."

"Will do." He set a pile of files aside. "I'm glad you called. Have they found the boy?"

"Unfortunately no, but I have some questions about your father?"

I had his attention. "Go on."

"You said your dad was sick and then two days later he was gone?"

"That's right."

"What were his symptoms? Was he tired and weak? Did he faint at all? Did you notice if he had any cuts on his arms maybe?"

"I...my mother said he was tired. He came home from work and went straight to bed. He got dizzy a few times and fell, but cuts on his arms? I don't think so. I'm not exactly sure where you're going with this."

"My mother took a medicine that made her bleed easily. Daddy used to say he could just touch her and she'd bleed like a pig."

"That's an interesting description, but what does it have to do with my dad?"

"Why did you come to the historical society?"

He raised his left eyebrow. "Because my mother said you came to see her."

"So you weren't coming to the meeting?"

"I didn't even know there was a meeting." He checked his watch. "Listen, I don't want to be rude, but I've got a meeting in a half hour."

"Rat poison has a blood thinner called Warfarin in it. People take it if they're at risk of a stroke or if they've had a heart attack."

"I'm familiar with the drug, but my father wasn't on it."

I nodded and stood. "Thank you for your time."

"Wait? That's it?"

I opened his office door. "I'll be in touch." I closed the door behind me and practically sprinted down the hall and out the main entrance to the office building. I held my breath, praying my plan would work.

∽

I drove over to Charlotte Hendricks's house. She answered the door seconds after I knocked, dressed in yoga pants and a big T-shirt with her hair up in a clip. "Chantilly, please, come in."

I stepped inside cautiously, paying attention to any possible signs from a deceased teenage boy. I breathed a sigh of relief when I felt nothing—no cold air, no whisperings in my ear, no hairs on the back of my neck standing up.

We sat in her kitchen. She offered me a drink but I declined.

"Have you heard anything about my son? The police still have nothing, and I'm stuck in this house staring at his stuff and thinking I should be planning his funeral."

I eyed an empty bottle of Scotch on the counter. Her frazzled hair and the dark circles under her eyes weren't just from stress and lack of sleep. Charlotte was bombed. She walked over to a cabinet and removed a new bottle of Scotch, then poured some into her glass and drained it in one swallow. After the third one, she stumbled to the table and sat. "It's the only thing that calms my nerves."

I'd hoped to talk to her about the skinny blond man, but even if she knew anything, it was probably buried under a fifth of Scotch. She leaned back in the chair and cried. "When is he coming home?"

∽

"You want mustard or mayo?"

"A little of both would be great."

Del smiled as she headed back to the kitchen.

Thelma stirred a packet of pure cane sugar into her iced tea. "She never makes this sweet enough. I don't know why she won't take my advice." Tiny red bumps dotted her face. I tried not to stare, but it was hard not to.

"I don't think you should use that mask anymore."

She scratched one of the dots. "I think I just had it on a touch too long." She leaned her head back and pointed to her chin. "Is it bleeding?"

I examined the dots carefully. They resembled chicken pox. "Nope. No blood."

Charlie shook his head. "Her skin's perfect. I don't know why she does that to herself."

I shrugged.

She sipped her tea, leaving a bright red lipstick ring around her straw. When she finished, she pressed her lips together and some of the lipstick stuck to her teeth.

"I like your dress today." I folded a napkin, then told her to smile. "You've got a little lipstick on your teeth."

"Oh, bless your heart. You've got better eyesight than me."

Del walked over with my ham sandwich and fresh fruit. "Everyone's got better eyesight than you." She set the plate in front of me. "Tell her to stop using those face things, will you? I'm itching just looking at her."

"I can hear you, you know."

Del shrugged. "How am I supposed to know if she's got her earplugs in or not?"

I smiled and took a bite of my sandwich.

Del stared at me.

I covered my mouth and talked with my mouth full, a habit I'd had since I was a kid. "Why're you staring at me like that?"

Thelma patted my free hand. "She wants to know what happened at the cemetery, but we understand if you're not ready to talk about it."

"You can tell us or not, but just know the next time I go to that cemetery, someone will be carrying me in my casket."

"And that won't be for a long time," I said. "Please."

"You never know," Thelma said. "She could fall down dead any day now."

My jaw dropped and Del's eyes narrowed.

Thelma smirked. "She ain't getting any younger."

"I'm young enough to take that drink of yours and put it where the sun don't shine."

"It's your skin," Thelma said. "Maybe you should try one of my masks?"

I kept eating and pretended Del's head wasn't about to explode.

Thelma caught my eye and winked. "I've been watching *The Golden Girls* on the TV. That one Maude plays? She knows how to say what she thinks."

"You mean Bea Arthur?"

"No, Maude. The tall, manly-looking woman."

"The actress's name was Bea Arthur," I said. "Maude was a character she played."

"Bless her heart, she looks like my cousin Bubba."

Del tossed her towel onto the table, flipped around, and said, "I'm out," as she walked away.

Thelma's eyes widened. "Maybe we could do a séance for her? I might could get me an autographed picture for my wall."

~

"Have any of the kids on the team been approached by other teams?"

Austin was head-down, staring at his cell phone. When he didn't answer, I plucked the phone from his hand and tossed it into the backseat of my car.

"Hey, I was reading a message!"

"Answer my question."

"What question?"

I rolled my eyes. "Have any of the kids been approached by people from other teams?"

"You mean the lacrosse team?"

"No, the football team." I glared at him. "Yes, the lacrosse team."

"I mean, scouts can't talk to us, I don't think."

"Not scouts. People from the teams you're playing now."

"Oh." He shrugged. "I don't know."

Teenage boys are so helpful. "What about you?"

He shrugged again. "I don't know."

"What do you mean you don't know? It's a simple question. Either someone's talked to you about playing on another team or they haven't."

"Geez, Mom. You don't have to yell."

I kept my voice low. "I'm not yelling."

"I mean, yeah, at tournaments and games and stuff, they talk to us. Tell us we did good, we should check them out, that kind of stuff. But it's no big deal. Everyone does it."

No, everyone didn't do it. "Can you describe any of them?"

"Maybe. I don't know. Is this about Turner?"

"A few parents have seen some men hanging around the park."

"A lot of people go to the park, what's the big deal?"

"Everything's a big deal when a kid disappears. Can you ask around? See if anyone's tried talking to the players?"

He groaned. "I guess, but I don't think anyone will say anything. No one wants to talk about Turner anymore, you know?"

"I know this is hard for you. I know you miss your friend." I pulled into the parking lot and grabbed a spot close to the field.

"We're just trying to play hard so we can win. Talking about it all just stresses us out."

"Got it. Don't worry about talking to them, then. It's okay."

He climbed over the seat and grabbed his phone, then got out of the car and popped the back window open to get his gear. He walked toward the field without another word.

I watched Bill Chatsworth pull into the lot. He dropped his son off near the bleachers and drove away. I expected him to leave, but instead he parked near the field. I kept him in my line of sight, waiting to see what he'd do next, but he stayed in his car. A few minutes later, a black SUV similar to his pulled up next to him. No one got out of either vehicle, and neither of them rolled down their windows.

The boys chanted and ran laps around the perimeter of the field. I locked my car, stiffening as I passed the storage room and saw the padlock. I stopped, but I couldn't bring myself to look at the door. "I can't," I whispered. "I'm not ready."

Mr. Rogers was close by; I didn't need the padlock to tell me that. I felt his energy, the familiar cold air surrounding me. I wiped the tears filling my eyes. "Give me some time, okay?"

The air shifted and a warm breeze swept past.

I said hello to a few of the parents, paying close attention to who sat where. I kept my eye out for unfamiliar faces, the skinny man, or any man with a potato body. I recognized two police officers dressed in plainclothes talking at the other end of the bleachers. Tim Jacobs saw them too. I climbed over to him and sat down. "They're cops," I whispered.

He kept his eyes locked on the men. "You sure about that?"

"The chief told me they'd be here, and he said they'd be in a red Georgia shirt and a solid-color T-shirt."

His shoulders relaxed.

"Just don't say anything to anyone else, okay?"

"Got it."

I climbed down and walked around the corner of the bleachers, acknowledging the two undercover officers with a slight nod. "There're two black SUVs in the back of the lot. One of them belongs to one of the parents, but the other one doesn't."

They calmly walked toward the parking lot. I followed.

Both SUVs were gone.

The squat officer with thick forearms leaned toward me. "Did you get the tag numbers?"

"I didn't. I'm sorry."

"Thank you," he said, and they both jogged into the parking lot. I turned around and almost walked right through Mr. Rogers. I gasped. The ghost didn't smile like he usually did. He just turned around and walked toward the storage room.

My feet stuck to the ground. I knew he wanted me to follow, but I was afraid to go in that room. I watched him turn the corner and disappear. "Suck it up, Chantilly." I checked to see if anyone caught me talking to myself. "If he can go in there, you can too."

Don Junior stood in front of the storage room door.

"Mr. Rogers!" I pressed my hand against my chest. "You scared me."

"I know you know something. Tell me what's going on."

Anger tainted the desperation in his voice. What was I supposed to do? I couldn't tell him private information because his father couldn't speak. I also couldn't tell him his father was poisoned without any proof. I shouldn't have gone to his office, but I needed to know if his father took blood thinners. I needed to know they'd given him enough rat poison to kill him. "I don't, I'm sorry."

His father stood next to him. I didn't make eye contact.

Don Junior pressed the palm of his hand onto the bald spot on top of his head. "Why are you doing this? Why talk to my mom and hurt her like this?"

A tear fell from the corner of my eye, but I left it alone. "I'm not trying to hurt your mother."

"But don't you see? That's what you're doing. Her health's not great. She can't handle this. Please, I don't care what you know or don't know, just leave us alone."

The ghost took something from his pocket and held it out for me to see, then turned around and walked through the storage room door. I closed my eyes and leaned my head back. "Well, heck." I squatted down and removed the key from the box, then took a deep breath and exhaled while I unlocked the padlock. I held the door open with my back. "I have something to show you."

He pointed into the storage room. "In there?"

I nodded.

I flipped on the light and closed the door behind him, then smiled briefly at Mr. Rogers standing near the shelves. He rubbed the small, shiny, flat rock with his thumb. I leaned against a pile of storage containers and did my best to relax.

Don Junior stood with his legs hip-width apart, arms crossed over his chest. His neck and jaw were tight with impatience and anger.

I eyed Mr. Rogers, praying I was doing the right thing. Mr. Rogers stepped aside, and I removed the items on the shelf, careful not to touch the plastic container of rat poison.

I pointed to the container. "This is what killed your father."

He furrowed his brow, then dropped his arms and stepped closer.

I grabbed his arm as he reached for the container. "Don't. The chief was supposed to send someone for this. It could be evidence."

He stepped back. "Evidence?"

I nodded.

Mr. Rogers rubbed the shiny rock.

Don Junior held his fingertip to his mouth and then pointed it at me.

I held my shoulders back and mustered every ounce of confidence and strength I had. I wasn't prepared to have this conversation just yet. One in a month was mentally and physically exhausting, but two in a day felt almost impossible. "Two men, one I believe is connected to Turner Bennett's disappearance, put the poison in your father's thermos." I let that sink in for a second. "I can't say whether they intended to kill him or just make him sick. That's why I asked you about the Warfarin."

"How do you know this?"

"Because your father showed me."

He blinked, rubbed the top of his head again, and shifted left and right. When he pointed at me again, I knew what was coming. People like to point at you when they think you're crazy.

I shoved my palm out. "Hold on." I relaxed my shoulders. "I'm not crazy. I'm not hallucinating. I don't have a brain tumor, and I don't want any money from you." I leaned against the rubber storage bins and crossed my arms. "I can see ghosts."

He blinked, then laughed. When he raised his hand, I pushed my palm out again. "Please, don't point at me."

His mouth hung open, but he dropped his hand to his side. Mr. Rogers moved next to his son. Don Junior rubbed his arms.

Don Junior wasn't the kind of man who beat around the bush, and I didn't want to either. "Why is your father rubbing a rock?"

He scanned the room.

I coughed and pointed to his side. "He's rubbing it with his thumb."

The storage room door opened, and Chief Hagarty stopped halfway inside. "Chantilly?" He eyed Don Junior. "Donny?"

Mr. Rogers disappeared.

I pushed myself off the rubber containers. "Chief, we were just—"

"We think we found the SUV."

Bill Chatsworth pulled up and parked near the bleachers. He kept the engine running as he talked on his cell phone. Practice was almost over, and I had to act fast. I casually walked toward his SUV and tapped on the window.

He rolled down the window, said, "I'm on the phone here," and then rolled it back up.

I tapped on it again and smiled.

I couldn't make out what he said to the person on the other line, but he clicked the phone and tossed it onto his seat. He shut off the ignition and stepped out. "What?"

"I'm fine, how are you?"

He grunted. "What do you want?"

"The name of the guy driving the other SUV for starters, and if you'd like to tell me where Turner Bennett is, that would be great, too."

He blanched. "I already told you, I don't know where the kid is."

"Right. And the SUV belongs to?"

"What SUV?"

"The one I saw you parked next to before practice."

"I don't know who that is. They came over, asked for directions, and left."

"Right. It doesn't matter anyway."

"Lady, I don't know what you're trying to do, but leave me out of it, okay?" He pushed past me and charged toward the field.

I ran to catch up and stopped in front of him. "What if it was William?"

He furrowed his brow. "I told you I didn't do anything to the kid."

"Maybe not," I said as calmly as I could. "But I think you know what happened to him."

He glared at me with cold, hard eyes. "Looks like you're not seeing the coach anymore." A sneer crept over his face. "Might be wise to keep your doors locked at night, huh?"

"Is that a threat?"

He smiled. "You take care now, you hear?" He walked toward the bleachers, leaving me standing there, shaking in my shoes.

CHAPTER 8

"We're having ourselves a slumber party!" Thelma rolled her large plastic pink suitcase through my front door.

I moved to the side and let her pass. "Uh. Did someone forget to tell me?"

Del handed me a paper garbage bag. "It's the rest of her stuff." She flipped around and hitched a small bag over her shoulder, then walked inside.

My eyes widened and my jaw dropped. "The rest of her stuff?"

Olivia walked in last with her own bag hanging from her shoulder. "You think we're going to let you stay here after that man threatened you?"

Austin leaned against the den's door frame. "What man? What's going on?"

I gave Olivia my mom glare.

"Oops," she said, and scurried toward the kitchen.

"It's nothing, honey. Don't worry."

His eyes steadied on mine. "Should I call Coach?"

"No. Everything's okay. It was just one of the parents at the park. That's all. You know how some of them get."

"Which one?"

"Austin, please, let it go. Everything's fine. These three like to overreact, and they'll take any opportunity for a girls' night. Remember last month when Thelma's washing machine overflowed?"

"They all came here."

"See? Anything for a girls' night."

"Can't y'all stay at someone else's place?"

"Not until you're in college. They know I won't leave you alone at night."

He groaned, and as he turned back to the den, he said under his breath, "That sucks."

I smiled and headed to the kitchen, where I glared at Olivia once again. "Blabber mouth."

She pressed her fingertips to her chest. "A girl needs her tribe."

Del set up a pot of coffee while Thelma got cups from the cabinet.

"Be right back," Olivia said. She left the kitchen, and a few seconds later, I heard the front door open and close.

"A bribe? I thought we came here to stop that crazy man if he comes callin'?"

Del groaned. "When this is all over, I'm taking you to the doctor. A possum hears better than you."

I bit my lip and then helped Thelma with the cups. "Y'all didn't need to come here, you know. I filed a police report, and Jack already talked to the man." I smiled. I'd told Jack about the implied threat and begged him not to make a scene in front of the team.

Del laughed. "I bet that went well."

"He called me an hour ago after having a little talk with Chatsworth outside his house." I gave them a play-by-play of the conversation. "He said I don't have to worry about Bill, but just in case, he's got an extra set of eyes on my place tonight. I asked him if everything was okay, and he said, 'Let's just say he knows what a real threat is now.'"

"That man is my hero," Del said.

"Mine too."

She poured a cup of coffee and handed it to Thelma. "We're staying anyway. Someone threatens our Chantilly, we got to act."

I handed her my cup. "Define 'act.'"

Olivia walked back into the kitchen. "Where do you want these?"

I flipped around and gasped. "What in the—"

"Put 'em against the refrigerator," Del said.

Olivia carefully leaned three large shotguns against the side of my new stainless-steel refrigerator. "Chantilly will send me packing if I scratch her new fridge."

I stood in front of the guns and shook my head. "Who do these belong to?"

Olivia and Thelma stared at Del.

"Delphina Beauregard, since when do you own guns?"

"Since about birth."

"Do you know how to use them?"

She blanched. "'Course I do. I went hunting with my daddy until the day he died. I'm almost as good with a shotgun as I am with a cast iron skillet."

"You got one of those, Chantilly?" Thelma asked. "Those'll knock you clear into next week."

"There's one sitting right on the sink." Del shook her head. "How are you supposed to shoot a gun when you can't even see four feet in front of you?"

I rolled my eyes. "Y'all are going to get us arrested."

"Not if we're protecting ourselves," Del said.

Olivia grabbed a bottled water from the fridge. "We're a tribe. It's what we do."

I had no idea what this tribe talk was, but I'd deal with that later. "Bill Chatsworth is a bully, but he's not stupid enough to hurt me, especially after Jack talked to him."

Del picked up one of the guns and examined it. "Locked and loaded. If Chatsworth shows up, he'll leave missing a few important body parts, I can tell you that."

I just shook my head and plopped into a chair at the table. Thelma wasn't wearing one of her Dolly Parton wigs. Instead, she'd wrapped her real hair in a pink scarf that matched her pajamas. "You're not going to leave, are you?"

They shook their heads.

"Fine, but this isn't necessary. Jack's got patrol driving by here tonight just in case."

"Good," Thelma said. "That'll help with our plan."

"Your plan?"

Del pulled out the chair beside me and balanced the shotgun across her legs. "You send that boy of yours to bed. We'll turn off all the lights and split up. Two of us will sit in here and the other two in the den. We'll keep a lookout. If he's stupid enough to come around, we'll make sure he's sorry he did."

There was no point in arguing. They'd made their decision, and even if I wanted to, I couldn't make them leave. Especially Del, since she had that big shotgun on her lap.

"You know how to use one of these, right?" Del asked.

I nodded. "My daddy was a hunter just like yours." It had been too many years to count since I'd shot a gun, but I hoped it was like riding a bike.

"Good, then you and Thelma take the den, and me and the baby here will keep watch back here."

"No." I pushed my seat back, lifted one of the shotguns, and rested it on my shoulder. "You and Thelma take the front. Olivia and I got the back covered." If Bill Chatsworth was stupid enough to come to my house, he wouldn't show up at the front door. That much I knew.

Del opened her mouth to object, but I cut her off. "My house, my decision."

She sighed and stood. "Fine. Leave me with the old coot."

Thelma's eyes widened. "You really should love yourself more, Del."

Del narrowed her eyes at Thelma. "I was talking about you."

Thelma heaved herself up from the chair and shuffled to the two shotguns resting against the refrigerator. She examined them for a moment, then picked up the one she'd have to pump to use.

"Maybe you should—"

She pulled the forend to the rear of the gun in one swift move, then pushed the slide forward and positioned the gun under her right armpit. "Let's get this party started," she said, and shuffled toward the den.

It took a second for the rest of us to pick our jaws off the floor.

"Mom?" Austin met us in the short hallway. "Why does Thelma have a shotgun?"

"It's not a shotgun," I lied. "It's a BB gun."

"I'm calling Coach."

"No, I'll text him and let him know what's going on, okay? It's late, and I don't want you worrying."

He moved a step closer to me, looking past my shoulder toward the kitchen. "Mom, she's like a hundred and eighty years old, and she has a gun."

"She's not even eighty yet, and I told you, it's a BB gun. Now get to bed."

He stared into my eyes. "I should—"

I hugged him. "I promise, I've got this. They won't be here long."

Dear Lord, not only had I just lied to my only child, but I sent him to bed scared for his life. I prayed nothing would happen.

Olivia and I sat in the kitchen. We talked a bit and then she sat staring down at her phone, laughing every couple of minutes at something on the screen.

Del crept in and tapped me on the shoulder. "Any signs?"

I jumped two feet in the air. She backed up as I flipped around and glared at her.

She'd set the shotgun exit side down, using it like a cane. "Chill your britches. You want to wake up the dead?"

"Pretty sure she's done that before," Olivia said, keeping her head tucked toward her phone.

Del peeked through the curtain on my back door. "You hear anything out there?"

"Not a peep." I groaned. "I appreciate this, but come on. It's late, we're all tired, and this is really stressing out my son. Please, go home."

It took some convincing and a lot of guilt about Austin to get them to leave, but they finally did.

I sat on the couch in the den. As exhausted as I was, I was too wired to sleep. I closed my eyes and tried to relax. A cold air swept over the room. I peeked out from one eye and smiled at Jack's grandmother, who was waving from the hallway.

"Here's your chance, sweetie."

"Chance?"

My cell phone beeped with Jack's ringtone. *Are you awake? I'm out front.*

I switched on the lamp and texted back, *I'll unlock the door.*

We sat on opposite ends of the couch.

He smiled. "Did they really come with shotguns?"

My eyes widened. "How did you know?"

"Patrol watched them put them in Olivia's trunk. He was going to call it in, but he recognized Del and called me. I told him to make sure they went home."

"Did they?"

He nodded. "They're at Del's." He leaned back and stretched

his arms over his head. "What were they thinking? Do they even know how to shoot?"

"You should have seen Thelma pump that shotgun and prop it up under her arm. I about fell over from shock."

"Thelma?"

"If I'm lying, I'm dying."

"Wow."

"I know." I rubbed my arms and yawned.

Jack grabbed a blanket from the basket in the corner of the room and handed it to me. "I know you're not going to go to bed, but at least try to get some rest." He kissed me on top of the head. "I'll call you in the morning."

His grandmother reappeared after he closed the door behind him.

"Chance for what?" I asked again, but she just smiled and then disappeared.

~

I met Chief Hagarty in his driveway. "Did they find the SUV?"

"Not yet." He opened his car door. "Chantilly, you look exhausted. Go home. We'll find Turner. Get some rest."

"What about the rat poison and Don Junior?"

"You're putting yourself in danger. I need you to stay out of this from now on. Please." He didn't give me a chance to argue.

I watched as he backed out of his driveway and then got in my car.

Austin sent me a text. *Going to the field to shoot some balls with the guys.*

Is a parent going?

I don't know.

I called him. "I don't want you going to the park without adult supervision."

"Mom, please? We want to practice for the tournament."

"No. Not now. I'll get off work early and y'all can go before practice."

"But, Mom!"

"I'm not arguing about this." I disconnected the call.

I drove to work thinking about Austin and Turner. Turner's disappearance shook me to the core. Every time I thought about what happened, I pictured my son's face. But this wasn't about Austin, and as much as I wanted to protect him, I couldn't lock him in the house forever. And a good mother wouldn't have shoved her kid off to bed when a bunch of crazy women with guns invaded her home.

I pulled into the parking spot in front of my office and sent Austin a text. *You can go, but text me back who else is going, please. Love you.* I stuffed my phone into my purse, grabbed my things, and headed straight upstairs to my office, closing the door behind me.

I checked our voicemail. Six messages from Don Junior. I deleted them all. Jack called my cell, but I sent it to voicemail. I shot him a quick message and said I was fine but buried at work.

Olivia knocked once and opened my door. "You doing okay?"

"I'm fine. I just need a little breathing room right now, okay?"

She set a cup of coffee on my desk. "Sure thing. I've got the phones covered."

I glanced at my calendar. "I have a meeting with a homeowner in an hour."

She flipped the calendar toward her. "I'll handle it. Where's their file?"

I searched the folders on my desk and handed it to her.

"You haven't slept in days. Go home, turn your phone off. I'll tell Del and Thelma not to disturb you."

I closed my laptop. "I think I'll do that." I didn't bother packing my things. I just took my purse and left.

Olivia was right. I was exhausted. I checked my phone, but

Austin hadn't responded to my text. I clicked on the thread and saw that my message was delivered but not read. I called him. It rang four times and went to voicemail. "You were supposed to tell me who's going to the park. Please text me."

My phone rang. I checked the caller ID and answered.

"Charlotte? Are you okay?"

"Chantilly, it's Travis. Charlotte's not doing well."

"I can understand."

"I can't get her to calm down. She's been drinking, and she's bawling her eyes out right now. She's asked for you. I don't want to—do you think you can come by?"

"Yeah, of course. I'll head over there now."

"Thanks."

Travis opened the front door as I walked up the sidewalk. He looked like he hadn't slept in days. "She just passed out." He pushed the door all the way open and walked through the living room toward the kitchen. "At least I got her to bed."

Two empty bottles of Scotch sat next to the sink. Travis tossed them into the garbage. "This is getting out of hand."

"Her son is missing."

"I know, but Scotch isn't going to bring him back." He opened the refrigerator and took out two bottled waters, then handed one to me. "Have a seat."

I sat at the bar while he wiped down the counter. "The police are going to find him."

"I'm not so sure about that." He pushed a pile of papers to the side of the bar and set down his water. "It's been too long. Turner's long gone by now."

"You think Turner ran away?"

"I didn't at first, but yeah, I do." He sipped his water and pushed the pile of papers closer to the edge of the bar. "Charlotte's drinking has been out of hand for a while now. It got worse when Bennett moved here and started bugging Turner about moving in with him."

I glanced at the pile of papers, then back at Travis. "I didn't know she had a problem."

"I didn't think she did, but I was wrong. The night before Turner disappeared, he told her he wanted to move in with his dad. She was already drunk and it got ugly."

Charlotte hollered for Turner, and then something hit the floor.

"She fell out of bed. I'll be right back."

He walked out of the kitchen. I listened as he climbed the stairs and then moved the pile of papers and saw a photo underneath them.

My heart stopped. In the photo, four men posed with golf clubs in front of the Habersham Estates Golf Club sign. I swallowed hard as I stared at Travis Hendricks standing between the skinny guy with the baseball cap and a shorter man with a very familiar potato-shaped middle. I didn't recognize the other man. I stuffed the photo into my purse and rearranged the papers on the bar as Charlotte cried upstairs.

I walked to the front door and left quietly. I called Jack as I turned off their street. "Hey, it's me. I need you and the chief to call me, please. It's Travis Hendricks. He's done something to Turner. He doesn't know I know. Just call me, okay?"

I headed straight to the park to check on Austin. A black SUV passed me about two blocks from the entrance. I watched it in my rearview mirror, but it sped up, and I couldn't catch the tag numbers. My heart raced. Did Travis know the boys were going to shoot balls? Did he send the men to the park? I called Jack, tossing the phone onto the passenger seat when it went straight to voicemail.

The field was empty. I pulled into the lot to check the bathrooms and panicked when I saw Austin's bike leaning up against the fence. I whipped my car around and hit the gas. "Hey, Siri, call Austin cell."

"Calling Austin Adair, cell."

It went straight to voicemail. The SUV was nowhere in sight. I called Jack and got his voicemail again. "Call me!" I screamed into his voicemail, then opened my text thread with Austin and clicked on the info icon to check his location. "Route 53?" My eyes widened. I sped through a stop sign and took the next right.

"Hey, Siri, call Jack work."

"Calling Jack Levitt, work."

"Castleberry Police. Sergeant Miller speaking."

"Chief Hagarty, please."

"He's in a meeting, can I take a message?"

"No. Tell him it's Chantilly Adair, and they've got my son. Travis Hendricks is involved."

"Can you repeat that?"

"The men who took Turner Bennett! They've got my son!"

"Ma'am, where are you?"

"I'm trying to find the SUV. I think it's heading south on 53. Just tell the chief!" I hit end and refreshed Austin's location.

Route 53 ran parallel along several small towns in the area. It curved southeast just north of Bramblett County. A large developer from Atlanta bought several parcels of land and built a golf community called Habersham Estates Golf and Country Club.

I still didn't have the SUV in sight, so I sped up and passed the two cars in front of me before spotting it at the bottom of the hill.

"Hey, Siri, call Jack cell."

"Calling Jack Levitt, cell."

It rang once. "Hey, I'm—"

"They've got Austin!"

"What?"

"The black SUV. I'm following it. I think it's going to Habersham Estates."

"Did you see them take Austin?"

"No, and I don't know if they have any other boys. He...he was supposed to meet his friends at the field to practice, but no one was there. I checked his location, and I think his phone's in the SUV." I took a deep breath. "I saw a picture at Charlotte's. Jack, Travis knows the guys who killed Mr. Rogers."

"Killed Mr. Rogers? What're you talking about?"

"I don't have time to explain. Just tell the chief. He'll understand."

"Hold on," he said. "Black SUV. 53 south heading toward Habersham. Approach with caution. Boys might be in the vehicle." Then he turned his attention back to me. "Does the SUV know you're following them?"

"I don't think so. There are a few cars between us."

"Babe, I need you to pull over, okay? Just stay off the road."

"But I—"

"Chantilly, please. I gotta go." He disconnected the call.

A car pulled out in front of me. I slammed on the brakes and swerved to the right. My wheels hit the gravel and skidded partially into the ditch. Two black cruisers whipped past. I closed my eyes and took a deep breath, then refreshed Austin's location. He was still headed toward the golf club.

I yanked my steering wheel to the left, barely touching the gas. "Come on!" I gave it a little more gas, and my car crawled back onto the side of the road. I refreshed Austin's location and hit the gas.

A pickup truck barreled toward me in my rearview mirror. I tapped my brakes and pulled to the side, slowed enough to let it pass, then got behind it. Yes, Jack had told me to stay off the road, but no mother in her right mind would listen when she'd just let her son get abducted by killers.

CHAPTER 9

Two police cars sped past me. I sped up and down three more hills, slowing to a stop just a few feet away from a policeman standing in the middle of the road.

He walked over. "I'm going to need you to find another route, ma'am."

I stuffed my phone in my pants pocket, put my car in park, and pushed the officer out of the way with my car door. "My son's in that SUV."

"Your son?"

The police cars and black cruisers blocked the SUV. Jack's pickup was on the side of the road. I headed toward it, but the police officer moved in front of me.

"Get back in your vehicle, ma'am." He walked toward me, forcing me to back up. I darted to the right and raced toward the cars.

Jack grabbed my arm and swung me around to face him. His nostrils flared. "Get in my truck and keep your head down."

I did as he asked, keeping my head just low enough to still be able to see. The officers crouched behind their open doors and someone yelled for the driver to exit the vehicle. My cell phone buzzed in my pants pocket. The SUV's front doors opened and a pair of arms stretched out from each side. Two men slowly climbed out of the vehicle with their arms up in the air. I recognized them immediately. Two officers were on them in seconds, dropping them to the ground while two other officers stood with their guns aimed right at them.

They kept them like that as Jack and another officer checked the rest of the vehicle. I held my breath, waiting for my son to climb out, but he didn't. He wasn't in the SUV. I grabbed my phone and checked his location. His phone was in that SUV, but he wasn't. I knew exactly where to go.

I climbed into the driver's seat of Jack's pickup, adjusted it so I could reach the pedals, and then hit the gas hard as I yanked the steering wheel to the left. Gravel and dust clouded my rear view, but that didn't stop me as I sped past the trapped SUV.

I pulled up to the security gate at the entrance to the golf community. "I need to talk to someone about golf lessons, please."

The security guard pressed a button and the gate opened. I hit the gas and took the long paved road straight to the country club building. I skidded to a stop, yanked Jack's keys from the ignition, and grabbed the gun he stored in the glove compartment. I stuffed it into my purse and headed inside.

The receptionist greeted me with a smile. "Hey, you're here about golf lessons?"

"Yes. My friend Travis Hendricks recommended y'all," I lied.

Her face brightened. "Travis is one of our favorite members. Stan gives him lessons, though I don't see why. Travis has a great handicap. He doesn't really need lessons. Would you like me to make you an appointment with Stan?"

I furrowed my brow. "Travis had a little get-together a few weeks ago. He introduced me to the man he thought I should work with." I shook my head. "I got his card, but I lost it, and I can't remember his name. I'm sure I'd recognize him, though. Do you have a picture?"

She smiled again. "Sure do. We have tons of photos on the walls of the pro shop." She pointed to the hallway. "I'll tell you what. Go have yourself a look, and if you see the man, just bring the photo on back to me. I'll get you set right up."

Bingo, I thought. I thanked her and left.

I examined every photo carefully until I found one I recognized. It was the exact same photo as the one in my purse. "Excuse me," I said to the cashier. "Do you know who this man is?" I pointed to the man I didn't recognize.

"Yeah, that's Brad Meyer. He's the boss here."

I smiled and kept my voice calm as my phone rang in my purse. "Is he here today?"

"Sure is. Take a left and head down the hall. He's the third door on the left."

"Thanks," I said.

As I headed out of the pro shop, the receptionist stopped me. "Oh, wait. He's not there. He went to the storage room in the basement. He'll be back in a bit, though, if you want to wait."

"I'll wait by his office. Thanks." I opened every door in that hallway, but none led to the basement. I backtracked, ignoring my phone as it rang again, and ducked past the receptionist. Three halls and six doors later, I found the basement.

I stepped quietly down the dark stairs. A dim light under a door on the right cast a soft glow on the basement floor. I hid behind a corner, caught my breath, and then tiptoed toward the door.

"Just shut up," a man said.

I stepped over the light on the floor and flattened my back against the wall. I carefully removed my phone and put it on silent. Six missed calls, all from Jack. I pulled up our text thread and shared my location with him. He responded immediately. *Almost there.*

I texted back, *Basement. Brad Meyer. Manager.* My heart was pumping so hard I could barely breathe. I caught my breath and squinted as my eyes adjusted to the dark.

Shelves filled with boxes of golf equipment lined the wall opposite me. A few feet away I found my weapon of choice. I could shoot Jack's gun, but I couldn't risk hurting my child. I picked the golf club with the biggest head, stepped back to the door, and waited.

The door opened, and Austin's voice was strong and determined. "Coach will find us!"

"Just keep your mouth shut, and I'll let you live."

I sucked in my breath and stepped out from behind the door, holding the club like a bat. When Brad Meyer walked out, I kicked the door shut and swung the club smack into the side of his head. He went down fast. The smack vibrated up the club's shaft and into my hands.

Brad Meyer lay on his stomach. I tapped him with the head of the club, but he didn't move. "Don't piss off a mother!"

The door opened and hit Brad Meyer's feet. I raised the club again.

"Mom!"

I dropped the club as Austin wrapped his arms around me.

Footsteps beat down the stairs, and the lights came on.

"Turner? Where's Turner?"

"In there," Austin said. I rushed to the boy sitting on a barrel in the corner. Tears streamed down his face. I pulled him up and hugged him as he cried into my shoulder.

"It's okay. You're okay." I pulled away and examined Turner carefully. "Did they hurt you? Are you okay? Does anything hurt?" A billion questions cluttered my mind. I blurted out several more without giving him the chance to respond.

Turner wiped his face. "I'm okay."

Austin leaned his shoulder against mine.

Jack walked into the room. "Paramedics are on their way." He checked both boys carefully. "Meyer's conscious."

The feeling of relief surprised me. "What about Travis?"

"Sitting in a holding cell as we speak."

Turner sat back down on the barrel. "Can I call my mom?"

Jack gripped the boy's shoulder. "Your mom will meet you at the hospital, okay?"

"The hospital? Is she all right?"

Jack smiled. "Your mom's fine. We're taking you to the hospital to get checked out."

I hugged Austin again. "You're going too."

"How did you know where to find us?"

"You're sharing your location with me, remember?"

He moved to the side and looked into the hall. "Whoa. You took him down! That was awesome!"

I laughed. "Never mess with a momma bear."

~

Travis's arrest and the knowledge that her son was okay sobered Charlotte up fast. "Where's my boy?"

I tucked the hospital bed sheet around Austin's legs. "She's loud."

He laughed. "My mom's the stealth mom with a good swing."

Thank God my son had a sense of humor. I poked his chest lightly. "Remember that before you sass me again, you hear?"

His smile faded. "Why did Mr. Hendricks do this?"

I sat on the side of the bed. "I don't know, but Jack's handling everything now, and he promised to let me know what's going on. I don't want you worrying about this now, though, okay? You need to rest."

"I'm fine, Mom. I told you, they didn't do anything to me." He'd filled me in on what happened in the ambulance.

He was the first to get to the field. While he practiced shooting on goal, Travis Hendricks had shown up and told him they'd found Turner. He asked Austin to go with him, and when he said he'd need to call me, Travis said he'd take care of it. As Travis tossed Austin's lacrosse bag in his trunk, the black SUV pulled up, and the two men grabbed Austin, threw him in the truck, and took off.

Austin stayed calm while he told me everything. My blood boiled, but I stayed calm too.

They'd taken his phone and thrown it into the back of the truck. For the first time since he got the thing, I was relieved he kept it on silent. Had they turned it off, I wouldn't have been able to track his location.

John Bennett peeked around the white privacy curtain. "How's he doing?" His face was red, and his eyes were swollen. I walked to him and hugged him. He could be a real jerk, but I understood how he felt.

I wiped my eyes with a tissue. "Good. He's—"

"I'm okay, Mr. Bennett. How's Turner?"

At least one of us could hold it together.

"He's doing fine, son. Don't you worry about him. You just take care of yourself and your mom here."

"Yes, sir."

John whispered, "Doctor wants to keep him overnight. We're staying here with him. Coach Jack said he'd make sure you two are okay, but if you need anything, give me a call. You saved my kid. I'll never be able to repay that."

I laughed. "How about using my redesign plans for your house?"

He laughed too. "You got it."

The doctor examined Austin and released him. I stood outside the privacy curtain so he could dress. When the electric doors opened and Jack saw me, he smiled. But I needed more than that. I rushed into his arms. He lifted me off my feet and squeezed tight. He set me down, and a nurse giggled as she walked past.

I blushed. "I thought you were at the station?"

"I called the hospital and found out they'd released Austin. Since your car's sitting on the side of 53, I figured you'd need a ride home."

"They told you he'd been released?"

"I know a few people here."

He wrapped his arm around my waist, and we stepped around the curtain.

Austin ate most of the white chicken chili while I watched.

"Mom, you don't have to babysit me."

"I'm probably never going to let you out of my sight again."

He laughed, but I wasn't kidding.

"Don't laugh. I could have Thelma keep watch with that shotgun under her arm."

"You said it was a BB gun."

"I lied."

He smiled again. "I know." He rinsed out his bowl and put it in the dishwasher.

I checked his forehead.

He pushed my hand away. "I don't have a fever, Mom. Stop."

"Then why'd you just put your dish in the dishwasher?"

He rolled his eyes. "Night, Mom." He hugged me. "Love you."

I changed into comfy sweats and a big T-shirt and curled up on the couch with a soft blanket. I would have loved to sleep, but my mind wouldn't shut down. Even though Turner was safe, things were far from over.

Jack wouldn't forget what I said, and if the chief had solid evidence connecting the two men to Donald Rogers's murder, he'd want to know how I knew. And I had no idea what to tell him. Mr. Rogers would be waiting for answers too, and I'd also have to figure out what to say to his son.

I closed my eyes for just a second, but that second turned into hours.

"Mom? Are you awake?"

I opened my eyes slowly. "What time is it?"

"Ten."

"Really?" Cooper crawled onto my lap and meowed.

"I can't find his food. He's been bugging me forever."

I rubbed my eyes. "It's behind the paper towels in the pantry."

"I looked there."

"Look again. It's there."

His shoulders sank, and as he walked out of the den, he mumbled, "It's not there," under his breath.

I counted to ten.

"It wasn't there a second ago!"

Yep, Austin was just fine.

I took an extra-long shower, letting the water beat down on me and begging it to wash away the intensity of the past few days. I finished getting ready, picking out a pair of dark capri jeans and a lavender blouse for the day.

Austin talked with his mouth full of Frosted Flakes. "You're going to work like that?"

"What's wrong with how I look?"

"Nothing. You just usually dress fancy."

"I dress fancy? You keep talking like that and you'll have the girls falling all over you."

"Really?"

"Not at all."

The doorbell rang. Austin went to stand and then stopped. Maybe he wasn't as okay as I'd hoped.

"I've got it," I said.

I popped up on my tiptoes and checked the small window before opening the door. "Hey."

Jack smiled. "How's Austin?"

"Okay." I pushed the door open farther and stepped aside. "Come on in."

Austin glanced into the hall. "Coach!"

Jack studied him carefully. "You get any sleep?"

"Yeah. Are we still playing in the tournament this weekend?"

Jack took a deep breath and exhaled. "What do you think we should do?"

"I think we should play."

"Do me a favor, send a text out to the team and see what they all think, okay?"

"Should I send it to Turner too?"

"Let's let Turner get out of the hospital first before we talk to him, okay?"

"Sure."

Jack and I sat in the den.

"So, what's going on?" I asked.

"Brad Meyer was released from the hospital late last night. He's currently resting, probably not so comfortably, in one of our two jail cells. The other two, Chip Merriweather and David Brunswick, are at Forsyth County. Meyer will go there too, once we've finished questioning him."

"And Travis?"

"Travis Hendricks spent the night cuffed to a metal chair. They're all going away for a long time."

"That's good. They should."

"Merriweather's prints were a match for a container of rat poison hidden in the storage room at the park."

"Oh."

"Chief's talking to the district attorney about homicide charges."

I bit my lip.

"You told me the men who took the boys were the same men who killed Don Rogers. How could you know that?"

I ignored Jack's grandmother waving from the corner. "His son."

"His son?"

I nodded. "Yes. He was at the meeting, remember? When Amanda said she saw the skinny guy, he recognized the description. He told me his father was being harassed by the same guy."

"And he said they killed his father?"

"Well, not exactly, but he told me how his dad was weak and dizzy, so when I saw the rat poison in the storage room, I put two and two together, and told the chief."

"How'd you get into the storage room?"

"I...the door was open during practice one night, so I checked to make sure everything was okay, and that's when I found it."

He furrowed his brow. "Why would Rogers show up at the meeting about Turner in the first place?"

"I'm sure someone told him. He probably thought it might be connected to the harassment and wanted to check it out."

"Right."

Austin popped into the room. "Can I go shoot with the guys?"

My eyes widened. "You're not serious."

"Mr. Jacobs and Mr. Anderson are going."

I looked at Jack.

"Anderson's an ex-marine."

"I'm driving you."

"Cool!" He zipped around and ran to his room.

"Oh wait, his lacrosse bag is in Travis's trunk," I said.

"I got it last night. It's in my truck. Tell you what." He stood. "I'll drive him and hang out for a few minutes until everyone gets there."

"Don't you have to get back to the station?"

He smiled. "Hendricks isn't going anywhere."

Del slid my coffee across the counter. "You know lying ain't gonna get you into heaven. When are you going to tell that man the truth?"

"I'm hoping never?"

Thelma used a chair as a walker. Its legs scratched a path from the table to the counter. "I never lied to my Charlie."

"Woman, I just got the floors fixed from the last time you scratched them all up. I'm going to start charging you extra to pay for them."

"Oh, keep your pants on, Del. You can fix a floor, but there's no mending a broken heart." She wiggled her finger at me. I counted that as my first finger pointing of the day. "You tell that man the truth. Keeping secrets and telling lies won't keep you warm at night."

"Yes, ma'am."

She turned around and shuffled toward the door, leaving her chair next to me. Another customer held it open for her. "Thank you, sir." Thelma turned around, patted the dried bumps on her face, and smiled. "You tell my Charlie to git. I'm not dying anytime soon."

I looked at Charlie and mouthed, "She can see you?"

He shrugged and disappeared.

I stood and stared at the door. Del stepped beside me and nodded. "It's the wigs."

I unlocked the padlock on the storage room door and waited inside.

The door opened slowly a few minutes later. "Chantilly?"

"I'm here, Chief."

Steve Hagarty and Don Junior entered the room. The chief closed the door behind them. Don wore casual clothes and an Atlanta Braves baseball cap, a clear indication he'd taken the day off.

I acknowledged the cap with a nod. "Thanks for coming."

"I can't believe I'm here."

The chief patted him on the back. "Like I said, she's the real deal, Donny. Just give her a chance."

Mr. Rogers appeared next to his son. I motioned for the chief to stand with me. "He's here."

Don Junior rubbed his arms. "How does this work?"

"I'm no expert at it, trust me. But the few times I've done this, it's been like the chief explained. The spirit will tell me something I wouldn't know. It's called validating, but I don't like to use all the professional terms."

"Professional?"

I shrugged. "Your dad wasn't much of a talker, was he?"

"Did he tell you that?"

I laughed. "He hasn't spoken a word since I first saw him."

"And you expect me to believe he's here? Now?"

Mr. Rogers held out the rock and a gold cross.

"Was the stress rock yours or his?"

"Mine."

"Did you put it in his casket?"

"Is he telling you all this?"

"No, but spirits like to carry the items their loved ones left with them. What about the gold cross?"

He wiped a tear from his cheek. "My mom's."

I smiled at Mr. Rogers. "It's okay. The men are in jail, and Turner's safe with his parents. All because of you." I hoped he'd finally speak, but he didn't. "I'm sorry, he's still not talking, but if you'd like to say anything, he can hear you."

He opened his mouth to speak, but closed it and shook his

head. Chief Hagarty walked to him and put his arm around his shoulder. "It's okay, son. You don't have to say it. He knows."

I held my fist to my mouth and swallowed the lump in my throat. It couldn't end for them this way. They both needed peace. They needed closure.

"Mr. Rogers, please. I would give anything for a message from my father."

"Où sont les toilettes."

He spoke so softly I couldn't make out what he said. "I couldn't quite hear you."

"Où sont les toilettes."

"Is that Spanish?" I sighed. "He's talking in a foreign language. Something about toilets, maybe?"

Don Junior laughed. "Où sont les toilettes. It's French. It means where is the toilet." He laughed again, so hard the second time the rest of us laughed too.

"I've been trying to get him to talk for days, and when he does, he speaks French."

"My junior year of high school I brought home a flyer about exchange students. I begged my parents to host one from France."

I raised an eyebrow.

"I was sixteen. What sixteen-year-old boy wouldn't want a French girl living in his house?"

"Bless your heart."

He laughed. "That's what my mother says every time we tell this story."

"I'd guess she's thinking something else too."

He laughed. "Anyway, Dad said he'd consider it if I took the time to learn the language."

"Did you?"

"I nailed asking about the toilets, but that's about it."

"So, no French exchange student."

"Never happened."

Mr. Rogers smiled at me.

I knew what was coming, and I had to gather my strength to tell his son. "It's time for him to go."

"Go? No. I need to tell him I love him."

"You just did."

"Dad, wait."

Mr. Rogers's fingers trailed down the side of his son's face, and then he disappeared.

CHAPTER 10

"You haven't missed your chance, but you have to tell him."

Jack's grandmother and I sat on his front porch swing. It wasn't a windy night, and I wasn't pushing the swing with my feet, but it swung anyway.

"I know."

"Everything's going to be just fine, you'll see. My grandbaby is a free thinker, and he loves you."

"You know we're not together anymore, right?"

"Sweetie, nothing can keep soulmates apart. Look at Thelma and Charlie. She may not see him, but she feels him. She knows he's there. Love like that can't be torn apart."

"I'm not sure Jack and I have that kind of love."

"Of course you do. When you zipped past him in his pickup truck—nice job, by the way, that's something I would have done back in the day—he made sure those bad men were taken care of and came for you and that cutie son of yours. You're his family."

Jack's garage door opened, its outside light brightening the driveway.

"You'll help me?" I asked.

"You just tell him his granny knows about that box. That's all he'll need to hear." She waved goodbye and disappeared.

Jack smiled when he saw me. "This is a surprise."

"I think we need to talk."

He paused and then unlocked his front door. "Okay. Come on in."

Jack's house was small but cozy. I sat on the couch in the main area as he removed his weapons and locked them in his gun safe. He kept a gun in his boot, but if he was home or at my house long enough to take them off, he'd leave the gun on the counter.

"I can't believe that's comfortable."

"Took a while, but I got used to it."

"I bet Officer Hansen doesn't hide weapons in her shoes."

"You'd be surprised."

"Is she mad?"

He grabbed a beer and bottled water from the refrigerator. "About what?"

"You're handling the case now."

"She's assisting. Chief wants me to work with her. He thinks we'd make a good team."

"You mean like partners?"

He twisted the top off his beer bottle and set it on the coffee table as he sat in the chair across from me. "Not for a while, but yeah."

"How do you feel about that?"

"It doesn't matter how I feel. Chief wants it, it'll happen."

"But he's retiring in, what, a few months? So he'd have to make the change quick."

"Anything can happen in a few months."

He didn't seem all that concerned about it, so I let it go.

"Hey, you okay?"

I'd been lost in my thoughts. "I'm sorry. I'm trying to figure out how to say what I need to say."

He set his beer on the table. "Just say it." Jack had downloaded a police siren to use for the department numbers that called his cell phone. When it went off, he groaned. "I need to get that."

"Detective Levitt." He listened for a moment, then turned away from me. "When?" He swore under his breath. "Did you put someone on him?" He walked over to his back door, unlocked it, and stepped onto the porch. I couldn't hear what else he said.

"Hendricks made bail," he said when he came back inside. He attached his gun belt around his waist and unlocked his gun cabinet, then checked his clips again and secured two guns onto the belt.

"How is that possible?"

"He's got a good lawyer." He stuffed the last gun into his boot.

"Where are you going?"

"To his house."

"Turner."

"And Charlotte. This is all about her."

I followed him to his door. "Charlotte? What do you mean?"

"I don't have time to explain. Do you still have my key?"

I nodded. It was at home, in my key box above the microwave.

"I need you to go home, get Austin, and come back here, okay? Come straight back here."

"Okay."

He kissed my forehead and then opened his door.

"Jack."

He turned around.

"I love you."

∼

I called Austin. His phone rang four times and then went to voicemail. "Turn on your sound!" I yelled. It was past midnight. Even if his sound was on—and I was sure it wasn't—he was more than likely sound asleep and wouldn't hear it. I checked his location and relaxed when it showed his phone at home.

The house was dark. Austin usually left the kitchen light on if he went to bed before I got home. I walked into the kitchen and heard Austin whimper. I froze.

"Turn on the light."

I flipped the switch. Austin sat at the kitchen table, and Travis Hendricks stood behind him with a gun in his hand. "Sorry for dropping in like this, but I just made bail."

I eyed the half-empty bottle of Scotch on my table. "Put the gun down, Travis."

He laughed. "Too bad you don't play golf. We could compare swings."

I held my purse tight against my side, feeling the weight of Jack's gun push against me. "You don't want to do this."

"I wouldn't be so sure about that. I had a good thing going until you went and messed it up." He grabbed the bottle of Scotch, took a swig, and slammed it back onto the table. "It's all your fault."

"I didn't make you kidnap your stepson." I flicked my eyes to Austin and prayed he'd stay still.

"I wasn't planning on hurting the kid. I saw an opportunity, and I took it. And it would have all worked out just fine if you'd kept your nose out of it."

I held my purse against my stomach.

Travis wiggled the gun. "Put it on the table."

I did as he said.

"All I did was connect the dots and find Turner." I hoped to keep him talking as long as possible. Jack would call me soon, and when I didn't answer, he'd worry and come over. "And my son."

He laughed. "Yeah, that was an unfortunate turn of events. But what was I supposed to do? You saw the picture."

"How about not kidnap my child?"

"Technically, that was Chip and David." He took another drink from the bottle. "Chip's kids play for the Hornets, and he's been stealing plays for years. He's willing to do anything to get his kid a scholarship." He took the bottle and held it toward me, the gun still in his other hand. "But you knew that already, didn't you? That janitor's son told you all about it, right?" He held the bottle to his lips again and stumbled backward as he drank from it.

I caught Austin's attention and mouthed, "Don't move."

Travis slammed the bottle on the table again. "They're trying to get him for murder. Can you believe that?" He laughed. "I figured kidnapping was his limit."

"Apparently not."

"In my defense, I just found out about him killing that man." He laughed. "But I'd still let him take the kid."

I inched closer to the table. "Why would you kidnap your own stepson?"

He laughed. "Why does anyone do anything? For the money, and Charlotte's got a lot of it. I've spent two years of my life trying to get to it, but I got tired of acting like I gave a crap about her and her kid. Merriweather saw my frustration and said he'd take the kid, we'd let people think he ran away or something, and when it all dies down, boom! We hit her with a ransom note and tell her not to contact the cops. And we were good to go until you saw the picture." He picked up the bottle again and drained the last of it. But he stumbled forward as he tried to set it on the counter.

"Austin, go!"

Austin jumped out of the chair and pushed Travis to the

ground. I kicked the gun across the kitchen and grabbed the cast iron skillet off the stove. "Call Jack!" I held the skillet and backed toward the table, my eyes glued on Travis Hendricks.

He pushed himself up onto his hands and knees. "You piece of—"

I held the skillet above my right shoulder. "Don't move, or I'll show you how good my swing is."

Austin stood behind Travis. "Coach is on his way."

"Do me a favor, carefully pick up the gun by the handle. Hold it away from your body with the end facing in front of you, and put it on the table in the hallway."

Austin looked at me, then Travis, before moving closer to him and kicking him in the butt. "That's for Turner!"

"Austin! Gun. Now!"

"Kids are like basketballs. You throw them on the ground and they bounce right back up."

"Under normal circumstances, maybe, but kidnapping and having a gun held to his head? I'm not sure the ball hasn't deflated."

Del handed me a coffee to go. "He'll be fine, you'll see."

An engine roared from outside. Del and I watched as a young man climbed out of a black pickup truck and jogged to the other side.

"Who's that?" she asked.

"Sam Merritt. He's on Austin's lacrosse team."

"And he's old enough to drive?"

"Most of the team's a class above Austin."

Sam walked back around the truck with Thelma on his arm.

Del rested her elbows on the counter. "Well, would you look at that!"

As Sam opened the door and held it for Thelma, I spied

Charlie near the front window. Little sparkles of light radiated from him as he watched his wife beaming.

Dressed in a short-sleeve yellow dress and platinum Dolly Parton wig, and carrying a large white purse over her wrist, Thelma looked like she was going to church. Only it wasn't Sunday.

She pointed to a chair at the first table near the window. "That one there."

"Yes, ma'am," he said.

I covered my mouth with my fist. Del didn't need to see my smile.

Del stood up straight and shook her head. "She better not."

Thelma patted his hand and handed him a few bills folded in half.

Before Sam left, he pivoted toward us. "See you at practice tonight."

When the door closed behind him, Thelma placed her purse over her shoulder, pushed herself out of the chair, and scooted it in front of her.

I rushed toward her and gently grabbed her arm. "Here, let me help you."

"But that's my favorite chair. It's the only one without any tears in the vinyl."

"If you scoot that chair again, you won't be worrying about tears in the vinyl."

She chuckled. "That woman's all talk."

"Better safe than sorry." I left her near the back table and went back for the other chair.

Charlie winked at me.

Del slid three biscuits, butter packets, and a variety of individual jellies onto a plate and set it in the center of the table. She poured coffees for Thelma and herself, then sat with us.

"That sweet boy told me what happened last night. How's Austin?"

"He seems okay, but time will tell."

Del turned toward Thelma. "How'd you get that boy to drive you here and walk you in like that?"

She pointed to the community bulletin board on the wall. "I called the number on the flyer."

Del walked over and read the flyer. "And carting you around is an odd job?"

"He's saving for college. I'm just being neighborly and helping him out." She squeezed my knee and winked. "I hear you whacked that awful man with your cast iron skillet. I'd sure like to see the size of that bruise."

"I didn't—did Sam tell you that?"

She nodded. "Told me all about what happened. He even said he wished he had a momma as tough as you."

"I threatened him with the skillet, but I didn't have to use it."

"That's too bad. Anyone who kidnaps a child deserves a skillet to the head."

I wouldn't disagree with that.

Olivia arrived, but I told her I'd fill her in on everything later. I had an idea, and I wanted to get to work on it.

Charlie followed me out.

"I know you're worried about her."

"I am, though lately she's surprised me."

"She surprised me every day of our lives together."

"I'm sure she did."

"She can't see me."

"But she feels you. She made that clear."

He nodded. "Make sure she gets to the doctor. It's in the early stages, and she's not leaving you anytime soon, but medicine will help."

I tried hard not to cry. "It's Parkinson's, isn't it?"

"Yes, ma'am. I'm going away, and I need you to take care of her, okay?"

"Oh, Charlie."

"It's the right thing to do. She's always talking to me, but I figured that was just her hoping I could hear. I didn't know she could feel me like she does."

"I don't know what to say."

"Just promise you'll take care of her. When the time comes, I'll see her again, but for now, I need to let her be."

I stood outside the historical society and cried as Charlie disappeared for the last time.

CHAPTER 11

The historical society board members sat around the large dining room table. "I realize this wasn't planned, and I appreciate all of you changing your schedules to meet with me."

Two of the members smiled and nodded. Olivia handed them each a file folder and then sat next to me.

"As you know, John Bennett planned to install a stone and wood verandah to his home. I provided him with an alternative option in keeping with the home's design. He also planned to install a small in-ground pool in the backyard."

One of the members spoke. "And we told you we wouldn't approve that."

I nodded. "Mr. Bennett is aware of that, and he's agreed to drop the issue. In fact, he's agreed to all of my suggested changes."

"Couldn't you have emailed this to us?"

"Yes, sir, but in light of recent events, I would like to suggest the board reconsider the pool." I opened my file. "I propose a small, square, in-ground structure with a limited stone and brick surround." I held up a photo, and each of them opened their files.

"While pools were limited to the larger antebellum-style homes of the era, I feel as long as it's small and in keeping with the design, Mr. Bennett's pool wouldn't disrupt the historical representation of his home."

"If we approve a pool for him, everyone will want one."

"Yes, however, Mr. Bennett's home is one of only three historical properties outside the perimeter of Castleberry's main historical area. I've contacted the owners of the other two, and both are willing to sign documents stating they're not building pools."

"What about the ones in town?"

"The lot sizes in the historical section of town don't lend themselves toward in-ground pools, and I would update the requirements to state specific lot sizes. With each of you signing off on that, I don't believe we'd have any issues." I closed the file. "Ladies and gentlemen, my son was abducted by the same men who kidnapped Turner Bennett. You can't possibly imagine how I felt while he was missing, but I know it's nothing compared to how John Bennett and Charlotte Hendricks felt. Turner Bennett deserves a break, and if he can find peace and comfort in a small in-ground pool, who are we to deny him that?"

I called John Bennett. "I'm sorry to bother you, but I've got some papers for you to sign. Would you mind if I came by right quick?"

"I'm at Charlotte's. Can you come here?"

"Are you sure? I don't want to interrupt anything."

"She'd be happy to see you."

When Charlotte answered the door, she immediately started crying and hugged me. "Thank you. Thank you for saving my boy."

John smiled behind her. "Charlotte, let the woman breathe."

She wiped her tears. "Please, come in. Can I get you anything to drink?"

"No, thank you, I'm fine."

Her dark circles were almost gone. "How're you doing?"

"So much better. I've finally slept, and I'm pretty sure I used all the hot water in town when I showered."

"How's Turner?"

"He's okay. Sleeping a lot, but the doctor said that would be expected. How's Austin? Last night must have been terrible, but I can't say I'm not happy about what you did to Travis."

"I didn't hit him with the skillet, if that's what you think. I just kept him on the floor until the police came."

"He deserves a lot more than a skillet," John said. His hand rested on Charlotte's waist.

I blinked and pretended I hadn't noticed. "John." I handed him the file. "If you can agree to the redesign, you can move forward with the work."

He raised an eyebrow. "I told you I'd do whatever you suggested."

I smiled. "I know. Just have a look and make sure."

He opened the file and flipped through the pages. His eyes lit up when he got to page three and the pool. He looked at me with wide eyes. "Is this for real?"

I nodded. "It's not what you originally wanted, but I think Turner will love it just the same."

"You bet he will!" He shoved the file at Charlotte and said, "It's my turn to hug you."

He squeezed tight. "John, you're crushing my diaphragm."

He let me go and blushed.

∽

Jack and I sat facing each other on the Adirondack chairs on my front porch. "He didn't get bail."

"So much for that good lawyer, huh?"

He laughed. "He added another five felonies to his tab. The judge laughed when his lawyer asked for it. No one has to worry about Hendricks anymore. He's going away for a long time."

"I hope so."

Jack's grandmother appeared. She waved at me. "Hi, sweetie."

I smiled at her.

"What?"

My smile faded. "Just thinking about Travis Hendricks going to prison."

"Donny Rogers came by the station this morning."

"Oh?"

"Looks like you've got a fan."

I stuck my hand under my thigh. "What do you mean?"

"He said he'll never be able to repay you for what you did."

I bit my lip. "All I did was connect the dots." That was the truth. It just wasn't all of it.

"You did a lot more than that. You gave him closure."

"I guess."

He scooted closer. "I know why you came over last night, but before we discuss it, can I say something first?"

I swallowed. "Sure."

He exhaled. "I messed up. I don't need a break. I need you."

My heartbeat kicked up a notch.

"And it's not because of Hendricks and what happened. I wanted to tell you the night Turner disappeared." He held my free hand. "Can you give us another chance?"

I pulled my hand away. "Jack, I—"

He dropped his head and rubbed his temples.

His grandmother walked closer. "I told them all not to bury

me in this thing. I'm drowning in it, and the color does nothing for my complexion."

She gave me a lead-in, and I hoped it worked. Okay, I thought. Here goes nothing. "Jack, I need to tell you something, and I'm not sure you're going to want me back when you hear what I've got to say."

He steadied his eyes on me. My lip quivered as he gently ran his finger across it.

"You said I gave Don Junior closure, and I did, but it's not the kind you think." Telling the man I love I can see spirits was a lot harder than I thought, and I struggled to find the right words.

His grandmother stood next to my chair. "The dress, honey, tell him about the dress."

I sighed.

Jack leaned closer. "Chantilly, I—"

"Wait. Please, I need to say this."

He nodded and gave me that extra inch of space.

Tears filled my eyes. I ignored them as they spilled down my cheeks. "I saw his father's spirit. He showed me what happened to him. He showed me how he died."

Jack didn't move. He didn't blink. He just sat there, staring at me.

"Please say something."

"I don't know what to say."

"Now would be a good time to tell him about the dress."

I moved toward the end of the chair. "You don't believe me."

"I—"

I didn't give him the chance to speak. "You don't have to say it. I know the look. It's not like I haven't seen it before." I stood. "Let me guess. You're rethinking the break, right? For what it's worth, your grandmother really hates the red dress. And she's right, she's drowning in it."

His eyes widened.

I exhaled and did my best to keep my emotions from exploding. "I think you should leave."

He turned his head toward me but didn't get up. "Chantilly, I—"

"Just go."

"No."

"Give the boy a chance to speak," his grandmother said.

I crossed my arms over my chest. "I'm not going to try and prove myself to you." At least not any more than I just had.

He was up and in front of me before I could move away. "You don't need to prove anything to me." He leaned his forehead against mine. "I already knew."

He pulled me close. I wrapped my arms around him and cried into his chest.

He laughed. "Granny hated that dress."

I laughed too. "She's made that pretty clear."

I glanced around the porch, but his grandmother was gone.

He lifted my chin.

"How did you know?"

He kissed my forehead. "I'm a detective. It's my job to find the truth." He wiped a tear from my cheek. "And the chief sat me down this afternoon." He took my hand and led me back to my chair. "He told me about his son."

"He did? I asked him not to."

"I know, but he didn't really have a choice. He was there when Donny said you talked to his dad's spirit. He told me about the rock."

"Oh. Why didn't you tell me?"

"Because he told me you wanted to tell me yourself."

"And you were going to let me?"

"I was going to try." He smiled. "But I didn't know if I could wait too long."

"Honestly, I didn't have any plans to tell you anytime soon, but your grandmother is really pushy."

He laughed. "Is she here now?"

"No, I'm sorry."

The disappointment on his face was obvious.

"But I have a feeling she'll be back."

"Have you always seen them?"

I told Jack everything—when it started, how I saw Agnes Hamilton, my best friend's husband, and all the other spirits since hitting my head. I told him about Angela Panther, and how I went to her for help. He laughed when I told him Del was afraid of ghosts, and he wasn't surprised about Charlie.

He listened to everything I said, smiled when I smiled, and let me cry when I cried. He understood why I didn't want Austin to know, and he agreed to keep my secret.

The team won first place in the tournament. Bill Chatsworth pitched a fit when Turner showed up ready to play, but calmed down when he suggested William start. He said William was better prepared and he wanted to do what was best for the team. I still didn't like the guy, and I disapproved of how he pressured his son, but I did feel a little bad for thinking he'd hurt another child. Eventually, I'd apologize, but I figured I'd make him wait.

I sat in the bleachers and watched the boys shake bottles of water at each other as they celebrated their win, and I prayed Mr. Rogers was finally resting in peace.

The End

DECEASED AND DESIST:
Chantilly Adair Paranormal Cozy Mystery #5

If I had a nickel for every person claiming to be haunted, I'd never need to work again.

I've learned that not every slamming door, every electrical glitch, and definitely not every faint whisper, is a ghost. Most of the time, in fact, those things are easily explainable.

Most of the time.

Just not this time.

Now I've got an acquaintance who swears she doesn't have a clue who's haunting her or why, and a ghost who claims she's haunting the person who killed her. And I'm pretty sure one of them is lying.

**Get your copy today at
CarolynRidderAspenson.com**

KEEP IN TOUCH WITH CAROLYN

Never miss a new release! Sign up to receive exclusive updates from Carolyn.

Join today at CarolynRidderAspenson.com

As a thank you for signing up, you'll receive a free novella!

YOU MIGHT ALSO ENJOY…

The Lily Sprayberry Realtor Cozy Mystery Series
Deal Gone Dead
Decluttered and Dead
Signed, Sealed and Dead
Bidding War Break-In
Open House Heist
Realtor Rub Out
Foreclosure Fatality

Lily Sprayberry Novellas
The Scarecrow Snuff Out
The Claus Killing
Santa's Little Thief

The Chantilly Adair Paranormal Cozy Mystery Series
Get Up and Ghost
Ghosts Are People Too
Praying For Peace
Ghost From the Grave
Deceased and Desist
Haunting Hooligans: A Chantilly Adair Novella

The Pooch Party Cozy Mystery Series
Pooches, Pumpkins, and Poison
Hounds, Harvest, and Homicide
Dogs, Dinners, and Death

The Holiday Hills Witch Cozy Mystery Series

There's a New Witch in Town

Witch This Way

Who's That Witch?

The Angela Panther Mystery Series

Unfinished Business

Unbreakable Bonds

Uncharted Territory

Unexpected Outcomes

Unbinding Love

The Christmas Elf

The Ghosts

Undetermined Events

The Event

The Favor

Other Books

Mourning Crisis (The Funeral Fakers Series)

Join Carolyn's Newsletter List at
CarolynRidderAspenson.com
You'll receive a free novella as a thank you!

ACKNOWLEDGMENTS

This book wouldn't be what it is without the help and expertise of Severn River Publishing. Special thanks to Amber, the glue of SRP, and Cara, my editor, who made my story read so much better than I ever could.

A big shout out to Lynn Shaw, my PA, who's been with me from the start. You're a fantastic cheerleader and a good friend.

And most of all, thanks to my readers. To say I'm appreciative of your support is an understatement.

ABOUT CAROLYN

Carolyn Ridder Aspenson writes sassy, southern cozy mysteries featuring imperfect women with a flair for telling it like it is. Her stories focus on relationships, whether they're between friends, family members, couples, townspeople, or strangers, because ultimately, it's relationships that make a story.

Now an empty-nester, Carolyn lives in the Atlanta suburbs with her husband, two Pit Bull-Boxer mix dogs and two cantankerous cats, but you'll often find her at a local coffee shop people-watching (and listening.) Or as she likes to call it: plotting her next novel.

Join Carolyn's mailing list at
CarolynRidderAspenson.com

CPSIA information can be obtained
at www.ICGtesting.com
Printed in the USA
LVHW042040290820
664253LV00006B/523